A BOOK OF
TEDDY BEARS

A BOOK OF TEDDY BEARS

Brown Bears, White Bears,

Gruff Bears, Kind Bears,

He-Bears, She-Bears

and

Very Little Furry Bears

Collected together by Elizabeth Teague
and illustrated by Peter Rice

NELSON

THOMAS NELSON AND SONS LIMITED
36 Park Street London W1
PO Box 27 Lusaka
PO Box 18123 Nairobi
PO Box 21149 Dar es Salaam
77 Coffee Street San Fernando Trinidad

THOMAS NELSON (NIGERIA) LTD
PO Box 336 Apapa Lagos

THOMAS NELSON (AUSTRALIA) LTD
597 Little Collins Street Melbourne 3000

THOMAS NELSON AND SONS (SOUTH AFRICA) (PROPRIETARY) LTD
51 Commissioner Street Johannesburg

THOMAS NELSON AND SONS (CANADA) LTD
81 Curlew Drive Don Mills Ontario

First published 1970
© this selection 1970 Thomas Nelson & Sons Ltd
SBN 17 211003 3

Filmset and printed offset litho in Great Britain by
Cox & Wyman Ltd, London, Fakenham & Reading

CONTENTS

ACKNOWLEDGEMENTS

We are very grateful for permission to reproduce the following copyright material:

FURRY BEAR by A. A. Milne, from NOW WE ARE SIX, published by Methuen & Co Ltd and by E. P. Dutton & Co Inc.

THE BEAR WHO WANTED TO BE A BIRD by Adele and Cateau de Leeuw, from READ ME ANOTHER STORY, edited by Eileen Colwell and published by Penguin Books Ltd.

TEDDY GOES HOME by Frances Lindsay, from MY FIRST STORY BOOK, published by Litor Publishers Ltd.

LITTLE BEAR GOES TO THE MOON by Else Holmelund Minarik, from LITTLE BEAR, published by World's Work Ltd and by Harper & Row.

THE STORY OF BELINDA BEAR by Cam, published by The Bodley Head Ltd.

THE TERRIBLE TEDDY BEAR by Walter Krumbach, English translation by Marion Koenig, published by W. & R. Chambers Ltd.

BROWN BEAR BUYS A BARROW by Elizabeth Robinson, from BROWN BEAR AND SKIPPER AHOY-THERE, published by The British Broadcasting Corporation.

BENJAMIN BEAR, STATIONMASTER by Ursula Hourihane, from COUNTRY BUNCH, published by Brockhampton Press Ltd.

ALBERT PLAYS THE DUKE by Alison Jezard, from ALBERT, published by Victor Gollancz Ltd and by Prentice-Hall Inc.

HONEY BEAR by Elizabeth Lang, from THE BOOK OF A THOUSAND POEMS, published by Evans Brothers Ltd.

HOW THE POLAR BEAR BECAME by Ted Hughes, from HOW THE WHALE BECAME, published by Faber & Faber Ltd and by Atheneum Publishers.

THE POLAR BEAR by Hilaire Belloc, from THE BAD CHILD'S BOOK OF BEASTS, published by Gerald Duckworth & Co Ltd and by Alfred A. Knopf Inc.

TEDDY BEAR by A. A. Milne, from WHEN WE WERE VERY YOUNG, published by Methuen & Co Ltd and by E. P. Dutton & Co Inc.

WINNIE-THE-POOH GOES VISITING AND GETS INTO A TIGHT PLACE by A. A. Milne, from WINNIE-THE-POOH, published by Methuen & Co Ltd and by E. P. Dutton & Co Inc.

PADDINGTON'S VISIT TO THE CINEMA by Michael Bond, from PADDINGTON HELPS OUT, published by William Collins, Sons & Co Ltd and by Houghton Mifflin Co.

MARY PLAIN AND ST BRUIN'S DAY by Gwynedd Rae, from MOSTLY MARY, published by Routledge & Kegan Paul Ltd.

TEDDY BEAR AND THE ALARM CLOCK by Aaron Judah, from TALES OF TEDDY BEAR, published by Faber & Faber Ltd.

TEDDY ROBINSON AND THE CHINA GNOME by Joan G. Robinson, from ANOTHER TEDDY ROBINSON, published by George G. Harrap & Co Ltd.

GRIZZLY BEAR by Mary Austin, from THE CHILDREN SING IN THE FAR WEST, published by Houghton Mifflin Co.

THE DOG AND THE BEAR by John Yeoman, from A DRINK OF WATER AND OTHER STORIES, published by Faber & Faber Ltd.

THE SHE-BEAR by Ruth Manning-Sanders, from A BOOK OF PRINCES AND PRINCESSES, published by Methuen & Co Ltd and by E. P. Dutton & Co Inc.

THE POLAR BEAR by Magnus Magnusson, from ICELANDIC STORIES, published by The British Broadcasting Corporation.

HOW THIS BOOK
CAME ABOUT

Not long ago, there was a young bear cub who lived in a forest. All the animals were his friends and he had never even wondered what life outside the forest would be like.

One day, however, he came upon a little group of strange furry creatures at the edge of the forest. Some of these animals were yellow, some were pink and some were blue, but most of them had fluffy golden fur that shone in the sunlight.

The bear cub was amazed at these strange animals, since they looked slightly familiar, both like and unlike the forest animals he saw every day. Suddenly the animals spotted the bear cub staring at them.

'It must be a real live bear!' shouted one.

'I've seen pictures of bears like that in books!' yelled another, not to be outdone.

'Come and join our picnic!' cried all the animals together.

But the bear cub was suspicious of these new animals. 'Who are you?' he asked them.

'We're teddy bears, of course' the animals replied.

'Pull the other leg' said the bear cub. 'You're not *bears*. You're the wrong colour, for a start. Real bears are brown. And no *bear* ever went on a *picnic*!'

'Of course we're bears' said the teddy bears indignantly. 'But we're not any old kind of wild bears living out of doors. We're special bears who live in houses with children. What's more, we're called teddy bears after Teddy Roosevelt, who was *President* of the *United States of America,* so you can see how important we are.'

'What's the Presi-wherever-you-said of whatever-it-was?' asked the bear cub, trying not to be put out. 'When *I* grow up I'm going to be a big fierce grizzly bear and eat people and teddy bears just for *breakfast*, so there! And I bet my life in the forest is much more exciting than living in a boring old house.'

'Tell us about it then,' said one of the teddy bears. 'Yes!' cried another teddy bear. 'Let's all tell stories! We'll each tell a story about our adventures, and the real bear can tell us stories about his.'

So that is how this book came about. At any rate, that is how it *could* have come about. . . .

FURRY BEAR

by A. A. Milne

If I were a bear,
  And a big bear too,
I shouldn't much care
  If it froze or snew;
I shouldn't much mind
  If it snowed or friz –
I'd be all fur-lined
  With a coat like his!

For I'd have fur boots and a brown fur wrap
And brown fur knickers and a big fur cap.
I'd have a fur muffle-ruff to cover my jaws,
And brown fur mittens on my big brown paws.
With a big brown furry-down up to my head,
I'd sleep all the winter in a big fur bed.

from NOW WE ARE SIX

I

THE BEAR WHO WANTED TO BE A BIRD

by Adele and Cateau de Leeuw

There was once a little black bear who wanted to be a bird. He wished it so hard, and thought about it so much, that finally he decided he *was* one.

Going through the forest one day he saw some birds high up in a tree. 'Hello,' he said. 'I'm a bird, too.'

The birds laughed at him. '*You're* not a bird,' they said. 'Birds have beaks.'

The little black bear scurried through the forest until he found a thin piece of wood that had a point. He tied it to his muzzle and hurried back to the tree where the birds sat. 'See,' he cried, looking up, 'I have a beak!'

'Just the same,' they said, 'you're not a bird. Birds have feathers.'

So the little black bear ran as fast as he could out of the forest and found a chicken yard. There were lots of feathers lying on the ground. He picked them up and went back to the forest. There he sat down on some pine needles and stuck the feathers all over his head and his shoulders and down his front legs. Then he went to the tree where the birds sat and cried happily, 'I have feathers, too. See, I'm a bird.'

But the birds only laughed at him. 'You're not a bird,' they said. 'Don't you know that birds sing?'

The little black bear felt sad, but not for long. He remembered that deep in the forest was a house where a singing teacher lived. He went there and knocked on the door. 'Please teach me to sing,' he begged. 'I *must* learn to sing.'

'It's most unusual,' said the singing teacher. 'But I will try. I have a wonderful system. Come in. Open your mouth.

Now follow me – do, re, mi, re, do . . . do, re, mi, re, do.'

The little black bear practised and practised and practised for a whole week, and then, feeling that he was very good indeed, he hurried back to the tree where the birds were.

'Listen,' he cried. 'I can sing, too.' And he opened his mouth very wide, and in a deep voice sang, 'Do, re, mi, re, do . . . do, re, mi, re do.'

The birds laughed harder than ever. 'You're not a bird,' they told him. 'Birds fly.'

The little black bear said, 'I can fly, too.' He lifted first one foot, all covered with feathers, and then the other, and then hopped up and down, lifting both together. But he did not fly.

'I must get higher off the ground,' he said. 'Watch me.' So he went to a big rock nearby and climbed up on it, and looked over the edge. The ground seemed very far away. 'But,' he thought, 'maybe if I take a running start, and don't look down, it will be all right.' So he backed off, closed

his eyes, ran as fast as he could to the edge of the rock, lifted his feet, flapped them – and fell, with a loud smack, on his little behind on the ground.

He opened his eyes, and felt the tears coming. It hurt where he had fallen. His beak had slipped off; feathers were lying all over the ground.

The little birds laughed and laughed, high up in the tree, and then they all flew away together.

'You're not a bird,' they called, and it floated back to him on the wind. 'You're not a bird, you're a bear.'

He picked himself up and walked slowly through the forest. He felt very bad, and everything ached.

He rubbed his muzzle, and was glad that the clumsy beak wasn't tied to it any more. He picked the rest of the feathers off himself, and his fur felt soft and furry. He found a bush with some beautiful red berries on it. They looked good, and he went over and stripped some off and ate them. They were delicious – much, much nicer than the worms that birds had to eat – and he ran his tongue around his black muzzle and pulled off another bunch.

After a while he met another bear, just about his size,

coming toward him in the forest. 'Hello,' said the other bear.

'Wuf, wuf,' said the little black bear. And he thought, 'I like the sound of that. It's much better than having to sing do, re, mi, re, do in a deep voice.'

'Come and see what *I've* found,' his new friend said.

He led him to a big tree and climbed it. 'Follow me,' he said, and the little black bear did. Up in the first crotch was a bee's nest and a big comb of honey.

'Oh,' said the little black bear, 'what a wonderful find!' He dipped his paw in the honeycomb and licked it. Then he dipped it in again and licked it once more.

'I'm *glad* I'm a bear,' he said. 'Who would want to be a bird, anyhow?'

from READ ME ANOTHER STORY

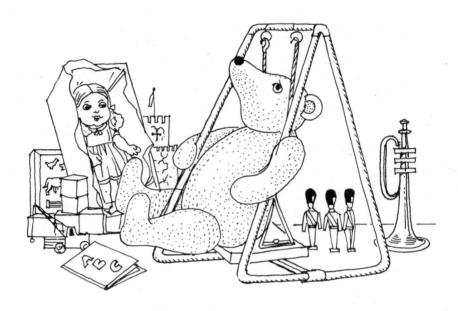

TEDDY GOES HOME

by Frances Lindsay

Mr Jolly's toyshop was a most exciting place. Every day little boys and girls would look in the window, pressing their noses against the glass, and wish that they could have all the wonderful toys they saw.

One day in the middle of Mr Jolly's shop window there hung a blue swing and on it sat a very special bear.

The little bear could squeak; he could say 'hallo' and he could say 'good-bye.' He was the prettiest little bear you ever saw and he was waiting for someone nice to come and take him home.

At last a man and a little girl came into the shop. The bear noticed that the little girl looked very cross. 'I hope that they don't want to buy me,' he thought.

'Show me that bear,' said the man without even a 'please' or a 'thank-you.'

Mr Jolly came to the window. 'I'll just take him out of the swing,' he said.

Teddy took a deep breath and felt the swing tighten around him.

'Well I never,' said Mr Jolly, 'he's stuck!'

'What a silly bear,' said the little girl, and stamped her foot. 'You can keep him,' said the man and went out of the shop.

'That's very funny,' said Mr Jolly, and gave another tug. Teddy let his breath out. 'Goodness gracious me,' cried Mr Jolly, and nearly fell over as the little bear came out of the swing.

He looked at the bear carefully and then put him back in the window, but without the swing.

The little bear sat for a long time before a boy came into the shop. He looked very spoilt.

'Oh dear,' thought the little bear. 'I hope that boy doesn't want to buy me.'

'Show me that bear, I want to hear him talk,' said the boy.

Mr Jolly picked up the little bear and pressed his tummy. Teddy held his breath. Not even a squeak came out! Mr Jolly pressed him again . . . the bear was silent.

'He's no good,' the boy said rudely, and ran out of the shop, slamming the door behind him.

Teddy let out his breath with a loud squeak.

'Bless my soul,' said Mr Jolly, and looked curiously at the little bear. 'I wonder if there is something special about you,' he said.

The next day a pretty little girl came into the shop. She smiled at Mr Jolly and he smiled at her. The little bear looked at her curly hair and pretty pink dress and he began to feel very excited.

'Please have you still got that dear little bear who was sitting in a blue swing?' she asked.

'Yes, I have,' said Mr Jolly, and sat Teddy on the counter.

'Please may I hear him talk?' asked the little girl.

Mr Jolly pressed the little bear's buttons.

'Squeak . . . squeak . . . hallo . . . hallo . . . good-bye . . . good-bye . . .' cried Teddy excitedly.

The little girl clapped her hands. 'Isn't he clever,' she laughed. 'Please may I take him home?'

'Of course you may,' said Mr Jolly.

The little girl tipped her purse out onto the counter.

'Squeak . . . squeak . . . squeak . . .' said Teddy happily.

He was so pleased to be going home with the dear little girl . . .

from MY FIRST STORY BOOK

LITTLE BEAR
GOES TO THE MOON

by Else Holmelund Minarik

'I have a new space helmet. I am going to the moon' said
Little Bear to Mother Bear.

'How?' asked Mother Bear.

'I'm going to fly to the moon,' said Little Bear.

'Fly!' said Mother Bear. 'You can't fly.'

'Birds fly,' said Little Bear.

'Oh, yes,' said Mother Bear. 'Birds fly, but they don't fly
to the moon. And you are not a bird.'

'Maybe some birds fly to the moon, I don't know. And maybe I can fly like a bird,' said Little Bear.

'And maybe,' said Mother Bear, 'you are a little fat bear cub with no wings and no feathers. Maybe if you jump up you will come down very fast, with a big plop.'

'Maybe,' said Little Bear. 'But I'm going now. Just look for me up in the sky.'

'Be back for lunch,' said Mother Bear.

Little Bear thought: 'I will jump from a good high spot, far up into the sky, and fly up, up, up. I will be going too fast to look at things, so I will shut my eyes.'

Little Bear climbed to the top of a little hill, and climbed to the top of a little tree, a very little tree on the little hill, and shut his eyes and jumped.

Down, down he came with a big plop, and down the hill he tumbled. Then he sat up and looked around.

'My, my,' he said. 'Here I am on the moon. The moon looks just like the earth.

'Well, well,' said Little Bear. 'The trees here look just like our trees. The birds look just like our birds. And look at this,' he said. 'Here is a house that looks just like my house. I'll go in and see what kind of bears live here.'

'Look at that,' said Little Bear. 'Something to eat is on the table. It looks like a good lunch for a little bear.'

Mother Bear came in and said, 'But who is this? Are you a bear from earth?'

'Oh, yes, I am,' said Little Bear. 'I climbed a little hill, and jumped from a little tree, and flew here, just like the birds.'

'Well,' said Mother Bear, 'my little bear did the same thing. He put on his space helmet and flew to earth. So I guess you can have his lunch.'

Little Bear put his arms round Mother Bear. He said, 'Mother Bear, stop fooling. You are my Mother Bear and I am your Little Bear, and we are on earth, and you know it. Now may I eat my lunch?'

'Yes,' said Mother Bear, 'and then you will have your nap. For you are my little bear, and I know it.'

from LITTLE BEAR

THE STORY
OF BELINDA BEAR

by Cam

Belinda Bear loved honey. She thought about it, she dreamed about it, and she was always looking for it even in the most unlikely places. Wherever she heard a buzz or a hum she looked for honey, and one day she poked her greedy little nose bang in the middle of a wasp's nest. The wasps were very, very angry, and the King Wasp said to his army: 'Attack that bear! Ready, steady – go!' And they did, and there were eighty-one of them. Poor Belinda turned and ran away as fast as she could. She ran and she ran until she ran into the house where Potiphar Punt the painter lived with a mouse and some rabbits and squirrels. Potiphar Punt was so poor that at that moment he was wondering whether to sell his fiddle, and he was very unhappy because he loved his fiddle more than anything. But Belinda took no notice of him. She just dashed behind the curtains to hide from the wasps.

Presently the wasps went away, and Belinda poked her nose out and asked Potiphar politely if he happened to have any honey because she was feeling very empty inside. Potiphar said 'Certainly,' and then told her about trying to decide whether to sell his fiddle. So Belinda said 'Why not toss up? Heads you do and tails you don't.'

Potiphar thought this was a very good idea; but when he had tossed up and it came down 'heads' he said 'Oh, bother!' and looked very sad. So then Belinda took her nose out of the honey pot and said he had better toss up again, and perhaps it would come down 'tails' instead. But although Potiphar tossed up again and again, it came down 'heads' every time. So in the end Potiphar decided he would just have to sell his fiddle. He got his hat and he put on his overcoat and after telling Belinda that she could stay in his house as long as she liked with the rabbits and the squirrels and the mouse, he tucked the fiddle under his arm and set off for the town.

Belinda stood watching him go, but when she saw how sad he looked, and when she thought how kind he was, she felt that she must go with him. So she ran after him crying: 'Wait for me! Wait for me!' Presently they came to the town and there was a funny little shop with lots of interesting things in the windows. Belinda looked at these, wishing she could buy them, but poor Potiphar looked at his old fiddle and thought how much he loved it. And then he thought that before he went into the shop to sell it he would play one last lovely tune.

He played a tune that went up and down and in and out and roundabout, and when she heard it Belinda's ears began to wiggle and her paws began to wave and her feet began to dance. Potiphar played and Belinda danced. It was the nicest tune you ever heard and the nicest dance you ever saw. Belinda and Potiphar were so happy dancing and playing that they never noticed that A L L the people in the town had come to watch! When the dance was ended the people cried 'Hooray!' and threw them presents. They threw pennies; and some of the children threw toffees or buttons (because that was all they had). It all came to T W O P O U N D S and F O U R P E N C E (not counting the toffees and buttons).

So Potiphar had no need to sell his fiddle after all. Instead he and Belinda went into the shop and had a lovely time buying twenty-seven tubes of paint (all different colours), eight brushes, six pencils and seven extra-special india-rubbers. And then they went to another shop and bought five pots of Best Heather Honey – and who do you think they were for?

When it was time to go home they had bought so many things that Potiphar could hardly carry them all, although Belinda very kindly helped him by carrying one of the pots of honey. The sun was shining and the birds were singing and it was a lovely day. To celebrate they had a splendid picnic. The rabbits and the squirrels and the mouse were there, and a robin-redbreast and some bees. Belinda danced again, a special honey-dance, while Potiphar played for her.

At last Potiphar said he must get on with his painting, and Belinda said that in that case she would have just a little more honey before she went to bed. Potiphar painted and painted while Belinda ate and ate till the picture was done. Can you guess what it was?

It was a picture of a nice greedy little bear.

from THE STORY OF BELINDA BEAR

THE TERRIBLE TEDDY BEAR

by Walter Krumbach
translated by Marion Koenig

Trot! Trot! Trot! Martin was playing at being a horse. Round and round the lilac bush he trotted with his bear, Teddy Grumble. He galloped and snorted and stamped and whinnied. Teddy Grumble smiled all over his yellow face. He liked riding a horse.

Woa! Martin was tired.

'I've got to go now, Teddy Grumble,' he said. 'You stay here. You'll be quite safe. I've put up a notice.'

The notice said: 'BEWARE! THIS BEAR BITES!'

A flock of geese came by. They stretched their long necks to peer at Teddy Grumble. But they could not read the notice.

'Fetch owl,' cackled the geese. 'Owls can read notices. Owls can read anything.'

When Owl came she stared at the notice with her big bright eyes. Then she polished her glasses and stared at it again.

'This fierce animal bites,' hooted Owl.

Flapping their wings, the geese ran away in a fright. They hurried to the farmyard to tell the other animals about the fierce teddy bear.

When she heard the news, the broody hen jumped off her eggs with a squawk. The cock, who was on guard, shouted 'Cock-a-doodle-doo' and the fat little ducks quacked: 'Oh! Oh! Oh! It is a wolf and will eat us all up!' Then – splash! They dived into a deep pond.

What a noise there was in the farmyard!

'Run! Run!' cackled the geese. 'There's a horrible monster,' gobbled the turkeys. 'It bites! It bites!' clucked the hens. 'It will eat us all up!' quacked the ducks.

The noise woke up the old turkey cock. He was so cross that he spread out his great round tail. But when he heard the noise, he shut it up again with a snap. Then, looking small and scared, he ran away as fast as he could.

'Oink! Oink! Oink!' squealed the piglets. 'Let's run away, too.' 'Humph,' grunted Mother Pig, for they were locked up in their sty. Mother Pig pushed at the wall with her big snuffly snout until snip! snap! crack! the wall broke and they were free. Off they ran.

The cock told the cat: 'There's a monster in the bush. Run for your life. It's got snarly teeth and a big bushy mane. It is sharpening its claws. Run for your life.'

Tom Cat did not wait to hear more. He scampered up a tall ladder and jumped onto a chimney pot. Then he pricked his ears. Was the monster coming after him?

The doves flew up into the air. 'Coo-roo! Coo-roo!' they cried. 'There's a monster in the farmyard. It's got snarly teeth and a big bushy mane. It is sharpening its claws. It has eaten up the cock. It has eaten up the geese. Run for your lives!'

'Baa!' bleated the goat with the curly horns. He broke through a fence and rushed away without looking back. He was so frightened of the monster.

Cobbler, the dog, ran to find the huntsman.

'Bow-wow-wow!' he barked. 'There's a monster in the farmyard. It's got snarly teeth and a big bushy mane and is sharpening its claws. It has eaten the cock. It has eaten the geese. It is bigger than a bull. Please come and shoot the monster dead.'

The huntsman took his gun and he crept toward the farmyard. Closer and closer and closer he crept. All of a sudden a twig snapped. 'Oh dear,' said the huntsman. 'I must get help. I can't shoot such a very fierce monster by myself.' And off he ran, too.

Then out of the lilac bush crept a little grey mouse. She was not a bit frightened of Teddy Grumble. She ran up his furry arm and on to his furry shoulder. She took the notice to make a nest for her babies and, before she left, she dropped a kiss on the tip of his furry nose.

Nobody ever saw that notice again. But when Martin came back, there sat Teddy Grumble, smiling all over his yellow face.

'Everybody ran away from me – even the huntsman,' growled Teddy Grumble proudly.

Martin hugged him. 'Fierce old bear,' he said. 'Fierce old bear.' Then, hand in hand, they both went home to bed.

from THE TERRIBLE TEDDY BEAR

BROWN BEAR
BUYS A BARROW

by Elizabeth Robinson

Brown Bear lives with his friend, Skipper Ahoy-There, in a little cottage by the river. Every day, Skipper Ahoy-There goes to the docks by the river mouth, where he works as a pilot and brings the ships safely into harbour. Brown Bear keeps the house clean and tidy, cooks the meals and washes the dishes.

One morning when Brown Bear was ready to go shopping he found that he had no money left. 'I shall have to go to the dock and ask Skipper Ahoy-There for some,' he said. He locked up the little house by the river and walked along the river path until he reached the dock. Here he saw big ships and small fishing boats, and of course, Skipper Ahoy-There's little tug boat. *Woo woo*, it went importantly as it guided a big ship into a safe place at the dock.

When the big ship was in its place, the Skipper came over to Brown Bear. 'Ahoy there, Brown Bear!' he said. 'What brings you here at this time of day?'

'I haven't any money to go shopping with,' said Brown Bear.

'Bless my soul, I didn't give you any this morning! I'm sorry, Brown Bear,' said the Skipper, and he gave Brown Bear some money. Then he said, 'I'm glad you came, Brown Bear. I saw our friend Mr Tink on my way to work this morning. He was off on a trip to deliver some pots and pans that he had mended, and he was worried about Mrs Tink. She has a very bad cold.'

'Poor Mrs Tink!' said Brown Bear. 'I will go and see if she wants anything from the shops.'

'That's a good fellow,' said Skipper Ahoy-There. 'See you later,' and with a wave of his hand, and a 'Heave-ho,' Skipper Ahoy-There sent his little tug boat skimming through the water. *Woo*, it went, *woo, woo*.

Brown Bear found Mrs Tink in bed, looking very miserable.

'I've dot a told,' she said, in a sniffly, snuffly voice.

'My goodness, so you have!' said Brown Bear. 'I will do your shopping, and then I will cook your dinner. I had better get you some cold cure from the chemist's. Do you want anything else?'

'Yes, please,' said Mrs Tink. Brown Bear got out his shopping list and pencil. 'Ready,' he said.

'A tid of beads,' said Mrs Tink, in her sniffly, snuffly voice.

'A tin of beans,' wrote Brown Bear.

'Half a pound of hab,' said Mrs Tink.

'Half a pound of ham,' wrote Brown Bear.

'A large barrow,' said Mrs Tink.

'A large barrow,' wrote Brown Bear.

'Dat's all,' said Mrs Tink.

'That's all,' wrote Brown Bear, then he said, 'I am a silly,' and crossed it out.

Brown Bear picked up his shopping basket and set off for

the shops. First of all he went to the chemist's and bought a large bottle of cold cure. Then he went to the grocer's for the beans and ham for Mrs Tink, and some eggs and cheese for himself.

'Now let me see,' he said, looking at his list. 'I have to buy a large barrow, and that's the lot.'

Brown Bear went to all the shops in the village, but he couldn't buy a barrow. He went to see his friend, Mr Mend-a-Shoe.

'Where can I buy a big wheelbarrow, Mr Mend-a-Shoe?' he asked.

'Probably in the village over the hill,' said Mr Mend-a-Shoe. 'Why do you want a barrow, Brown Bear?'

'It is for Mrs Tink,' replied Brown Bear. 'I don't know why she wants it. I expect it's a present for Mr Tink.'

'Why not take a pair of these lovely slippers instead?' said Mr Mend-a-Shoe.

'Oh, I don't think I ought to do that, thank you all the same,' said Brown Bear. 'I will go to the village over the hill, and if I can't buy a barrow there, I will buy the slippers.'

As he passed the fishmonger's shop, Brown Bear saw some lovely, juicy kippers on the slab. 'I will take some for the Skipper's tea,' he said. 'The Skipper loves kippers!' So he bought the kippers and set off for the village over the hill. As he went, he made up a little song:

> '*I've got kippers for tea,*
> *For the Skipper and me,*
> *'Cos Skippers love kippers for tea.*'

He went along, singing happily, until he reached the village over the hill. Then Brown Bear started to look for a shop that sold barrows. Standing outside a gardening shop stood the biggest barrow he had ever seen. It was yellow with red handles. He went straight into the shop and bought it. It was a beauty. He put the rest of his shopping in the barrow and started to wheel it home. As he walked, Brown Bear remembered his little song.

> '*I've got kippers for tea,*
> *For the Skipper and me,*'

he sang. And then because his legs began to ache and he was very tired, he got all muddled, and sang:

> *''Cos kippers love Skippers for tea!*'

When he reached Mr Mend-a-Shoe's shop he showed him the barrow.

'That's a beauty!' said Mr Mend-a-Shoe. 'Mrs Tink will be pleased. You won't need to buy the slippers after all.'

'No, no slippers, thank you all the same,' replied Brown Bear. Then he set off through the wood to Mrs Tink's caravan. He sang his song again, but as he was very, very tired by now, he got all muddled again, and this is what he sang:

> '*I've got slippers for tea,*
> *For kippers and me,*
> *'Cos slippers love Skippers for tea.*'

When he reached the caravan Brown Bear said, 'What shall I cook for your dinner, Mrs Tink?'

'There is some cold beef in the larder, and perhaps you could cook the barrow,' said Mrs Tink, in her sniffly, snuffly voice.

'The barrow!' said Brown Bear. 'Oh! Oh dear! Oh, I am a silly bear. I do believe you meant me to buy a marrow!'

'Yes, a barrow,' said Mrs Tink, in her sniffly, snuffly voice.

'Yes, er – a marrow,' said Brown Bear. He opened the door of the little caravan and Mrs Tink saw the lovely yellow barrow standing there. 'I thought you said a barrow, Mrs Tink,' said Brown Bear miserably. 'I went all the way to the village over the hill to get it! I am sorry, Mrs Tink.'

'Ha, ha, ha!' laughed Mrs Tink. 'Ha, ha, ha! Oh, Brown Bear!' She held her sides because they ached with so much laughing. 'Ha, ha, ha! I haven't laughed so much for years! I think you have cured my cold, Brown Bear. I feel much better, and the barrow is just what Mr Tink needs to carry his pots and pans around the countryside.'

When Mr Tink came home he was glad to find Mrs Tink so much better, and he was delighted with the barrow. When they told him how Brown Bear had bought it instead of a marrow, he laughed too. Then he said: 'You cured Mrs Tink's cold and you got me a fine barrow. You are a clever little fellow, Brown Bear.'

'I am, aren't I,' said Brown Bear. 'Now I have to go home to cook the Skipper's tea, and I am so tired!'

'Well, I'll tell you what I'll do,' said Mr Tink. 'I will push you home in my new barrow,' So Brown Bear curled up in the lovely yellow barrow, and fell fast asleep, and he didn't wake up until they reached the little house by the river.

from BROWN BEAR AND SKIPPER AHOY-THERE

BENJAMIN BEAR,
STATIONMASTER

by Ursula Hourihane

Benjamin Bear was just going to help himself to honey when he heard a loud rat-tat at the front door.

'Postman sounds very important this morning,' he said to his wife Tabitha. 'I'd better hurry and see what it's all about.'

He put back the honey spoon and went to the door. The postman was holding a large official-looking envelope in his hand.

'Something interesting for you today, Benjamin,' he said. 'I hope it's good news.'

'My word, yes!' said Benjamin. 'What a lot of grand seals it has. And look at the gold crown marked on the back! What *can* it be?'

'Must be from the King, I should think,' said the postman excitedly. 'I can't stop now, but you will let me know if it's anything extra special, won't you, Benjamin?'

'Of course I will,' said Benjamin Bear, and he hurried back to Tabitha. 'Just look at this envelope,' he said. 'It must be something very important. Postman thinks it might be from the King! Do you think so, Tabitha?'

'Why not open it and find out?' said his wife. 'And don't forget in your excitement, my dear, that the nine o'clock train is due in twenty minutes and you've still got your bedroom slippers on.'

Benjamin Bear, who was the Stationmaster at Half-way Halt, looked at the clock hastily. It was true. There were only twenty minutes to spare before he had to be on the platform with his red and green flags and his shining silver whistle, all ready for work.

He opened the grand envelope as fast as his paws would let him and drew out a large sheet of thick white paper. He smoothed it out carefully, propped it against the toast rack, and began to read.

Dear Sir,

This is to notify you that His Majesty the King will be passing through your station on Wednesday next at three o'clock.

Please see that all is in order and looking as nice as possible.

Kindly keep the line clear.

The Royal Train will hoot three times to let you know it's coming.

Yours truly,

The King's Secretary

P.S. You may wave both your flags together as it's a Special occasion.

P.P.S. I enclose sixpence so that you can buy a bit of extra polish for your buttons and things. His Majesty is very particular about polishing.

'Well!' cried Benjamin Bear excitedly. 'Whoever would have thought the King's train would pass through my station?'

'What an honour! and what a Special Occasion! Why! it's Tuesday today, Tabitha! The King will be coming to-morrow. Good gracious! we must get busy at once.'

'Where's the sixpence the gentleman said he was send-ing?' asked Tabitha. 'If you give it to me I'll pop down to the village for some extra polish. Though no one can say your buttons are ever anything but shiny, Benjamin.'

Benjamin Bear poked about in the big envelope and fin-ally pulled out a shining silver sixpence.

'Here you are, my love,' he said. 'Get the best polish you can and we'll dazzle everyone with our beautiful station.'

'Never mind the beautiful station now, Benjamin,' said Tabitha. 'The nine o'clock will be here in a minute and you should be on the platform. Here, take your cap and flags and run.' And she bundled Benjamin into his uniform jacket and out of the door. Benjamin hurried down the garden path and through the gate to the station platform just in time to hear the nine o'clock whistling under the bridge.

'Morning, Benjamin!' called the Engine Driver cheer-fully, as he slowed down and brought the train to a stop.

'Good morning!' cried Benjamin. 'I hope you've had a good run?'

'Splendid, thank you,' said the Engine Driver. Then he laughed. 'Did you oversleep this morning, Stationmaster?'

Benjamin looked surprised. 'No, of course not,' he said. 'But I've had a bit of a scramble to get on the platform be-fore you arrived. I had the most exciting letter, Engine Driver, to say the King is coming in the Royal Train to-morrow afternoon. Isn't that wonderful? I was so excited I nearly forgot the time.'

'My, my!' cried the Engine Driver. 'I should think so in-deed. You'll be busy today, Benjamin. Well, it's time I was off. Good luck to you, and don't forget to change your slippers when the King comes tomorrow!'

Benjamin Bear looked at his feet. He was still wearing his blue check slippers!

'My goodness!' he cried as he waved his green flag, 'what a thing to do!' He blew his silver whistle and the train began to puff slowly out of the station. 'I must dash straight home and put on proper shoes. Tabitha *will* be upset,' he said.

What a busy day that was for Benjamin and Tabitha! They scrubbed and polished and swept and dusted the little station till it was as clean as a new pin. Everyone in the village helped as best they could. The Squire sent down four green tubs with pink geraniums to decorate the platform. The schoolchildren made gaily coloured paperchains to hang from pillar to pillar. Old Mrs Postlethwaite from the Post Office lent her big flag that was only used on high days and holidays. Certainly Benjamin's station did look a picture. By half past two on Wednesday there was hardly a square inch of room on the long platform.

'We'll have the children in front,' said Benjamin. 'Then they can wave their flags and cheer better.'

The Squire stood beside one of his tubs, and Tabitha, Mrs Postlethwaite, and the schoolmistress each stood by one of the others. At the back of the platform, standing rather shakily on a large luggage trolley, was the Village Band. There was Mr Puffin, the trumpet player; Bert Banger, who played the drum; and Miss Popham with her flute. Benjamin himself stood on a small square of red carpet that led out from the Ticket Office to the edge of the platform. He held his green flag in his right paw and the red one in his left. His buttons twinkled and shone like stars.

'When do you think we'd better begin playing?' Mr Puffin whispered to Benjamin who was inspecting everyone.

'As soon as we hear the three hoots, I should think,' said Benjamin. 'Then you'll be going well by the time the train actually reaches the platform.'

'I hope His Majesty hears us through all the shouting and cheering,' said Miss Popham fussily. She practised a few twiddly notes on her flute.

'Don't waste your breath now,' Mr Puffin warned her severely. 'It would be a terrible thing if you couldn't blow when the train does come.'

'Hold the flag up well, Billy,' Benjamin called to Mrs Postlethwaite's grandson who had the honour of waving the flag while the Royal Train passed.

Suddenly, in the distance, they heard three shrill hoots.

'It's coming!' cried Benjamin. 'Attention, everyone!' Slowly the Royal Train in all its splendour puffed towards the little station.

'Hurrah! Hurrah!' shouted all the children, waving their flags as they cheered.

Toot! Toot! Toot! went the band. The flag fluttered, the Squire saluted, everyone clapped and shouted, while Benjamin waved his two flags furiously.

And there was the King, leaning out of his carriage window, his golden crown with its sparkling jewels twinkling in the sunshine, and a broad smile on his round rosy face.

And then, suddenly, and long before the carriage had passed through the station, the King disappeared! A gasp of dismay ran through the cheering crowds. Didn't His Majesty like their grand welcome? Poor Benjamin felt ready to cry. His two flags drooped forlornly and even his shining buttons seemed to lose some of their sparkle. The King hadn't liked his beautiful station enough to bother to go on looking at it while the Royal Train passed through. It was a terrible disappointment.

Then, when the last coach was almost out of sight, an extraordinary thing happened. The Royal Train stopped! And, a second later, before their astonished eyes, the train began to shunt slowly back into the station! Everyone stared and stared. As for Benjamin, he didn't know what to think. The next thing he knew was that the King's carriage had come to a standstill right in front of the red carpet where Benjamin was standing. And His Majesty was leaning out of the window beaming delightedly and calling, 'Bravo, Stationmaster! Bravo! This is quite the nicest station I've ever seen. I just had to tell the engine driver to bring me back to have another look, and to thank you and all these good people here for such a splendid welcome.'

Benjamin bowed low. He was quite overcome. Everyone cheered and clapped and waved again.

'And now I fear I must go on,' said the King. 'But before I leave I should like to make you a little present, to remind you of this happy occasion.'

Benjamin bowed low again and took the little packet the King held out to him.

'Wear these on your best uniform,' said the King, 'and may they shine as brightly as those you're wearing now.'

Benjamin stammered out his grateful thanks. The King saluted. The engine let out a shrill whistle, and, amid renewed cheers, the Royal Train drew slowly out of the station.

'What a wonderful occasion!' cried the Squire coming over to shake hands with Benjamin. 'May we see the King's present?'

Benjamin opened the parcel and inside was a smart leather case. And inside the smart leather case, on a bed of creamy white velvet, lay six shining gold buttons, each with a crown engraved in the centre.

'Oh!' cried Benjamin, quite breathless with delight. And 'Oh!' cried all the people when he held them up for every-one to see.

And to this very day, whenever he wears his best uni-form, Benjamin Bear proudly displays down his front the six gold buttons the King gave him. Be sure to look out for them if you should ever pass through Half-way Halt on a Special Occasion!

from COUNTRY BUNCH

ALBERT PLAYS THE DUKE

by Alison Jezard

Albert is a plump, friendly bear, who lives in the East End of London and always wears a cloth cap.

The letter plopped on the mat just as Albert was finishing his breakfast.

He read it through and then he read it again with growing excitement. His cousin Angus was arriving that very day to watch the football match that afternoon between England and Scotland.

The letter had taken several days to reach him and there was only about an hour before Angus would be there!

Albert dashed about tidying up and making his bed, then he grabbed his shopping bag and his leather purse from behind Grandfather's clock and hurried down to the shops.

'What's all the hurry?' asked the grocer, putting a packet of ginger nuts into a paper bag.

'My cousin Angus is arriving soon to see the match,' Albert told him. 'He has two tickets and he is going to take me with him. They say the Duke is going to kick off and I have never seen him.'

'You are very lucky,' said the grocer. 'It is very difficult to get tickets for a big match. I wish I could go.' Then he went on, 'I tell you what, shall I lend you my rattle?'

'Your rattle?' asked Albert, puzzled and thinking of babies.

'My big rattle that I take to the matches. You whirl it round and round and it makes a lovely noise.'

'Oh yes, I know what you mean. Yes, please, I would love to borrow that.'

Mr Henderson went through the door to the room at the back, where he lived and came back with a great big rattle, which was painted in red and blue stripes.

'That's beautiful! Thank you very much. I promise to take great care of it.'

Albert packed his parcels into his bag and turned to go.

'Wait a minute,' called Mr Henderson, 'take these for your cousin,' and he gave Albert a packet of Scotch oatcakes. 'He will enjoy these with some of that special honey of yours, if you have any left.'

'What a good idea. Yes, I have three pots left and I was going to have one of them for tea. Thanks again.'

Albert had reached home and put away his shopping when there was a knock at the door. He hurried to open it and there stood Angus. He was a little taller than Albert and he was wearing a small tam o'shanter hat and a bright red tartan muffler.

'Angus, how wonderful to see you and what a big surprise. I only got your letter an hour ago.'

'The post must be very slow down here,' remarked Angus. 'How are you Albert? You are looking very well, but I think you are fatter!'

'It is probably all the honey I have been eating lately,' replied Albert. 'Sit down by the fire and get warm while I make you a cup of tea.'

He put the kettle on the gas and poked up a nice cheerful

blaze. Angus settled down in the big basket chair and Albert pulled a wooden one up beside him.

They had a good hot cup of tea and Albert told Angus how he had been given all the honey and Angus told Albert how he had been given the tickets for the match by an uncle who wasn't able to go at the last minute.

'I came down on the special train they run and I shall be going back on it tonight.'

'Well, we'll have an early lunch and then I will give you a good tea before you go.'

Albert had brought in some fish and chips for lunch, because he thought he would like to give his cousin from Scotland something very English, but Angus told him they often had it at home, and it was really his favourite food, but Albert was not to tell Aunt Bertha that, because she would think that he ought to like haggis best.

The two bears had a good gossip about all they had been doing and ate their fish and chips in front of the fire out of the paper, as they both agreed that this was the way they tasted best and then Albert said it was time they set off for the football ground.

They went by tube train because Angus had never seen one. He was a little bit scared and hung on to Albert as they went down the moving staircase, but, by the time they reached their station, he had quite recovered and wanted to go up and down the escalator again, but there wasn't time and Albert promised they would go home the same way.

They arrived at the ground and found their seats, which they were very pleased to see were right at the front and beside the passage where the players came out!

The two of them looked happily round and Angus said he thought the only better seats in the whole place would be in the directors' box!

Just as they sat down a band came marching out on to the pitch and began to play music for community singing.

Albert and Angus sang as loudly as anyone and thoroughly enjoyed it, especially when they played 'Loch Lomond.'

When it was time for the kick-off, it was very exciting to watch the two teams running out from just beside them and forming up into two lines facing each other on the pitch. There they stood and nothing happened!

After a few minutes, as the players began to look at each other, a man came out and spoke to the two captains and the crowd watched as the three men looked round them and then the captain of the English team pointed and it seemed as if he were pointing straight at Albert! He was! The third man suddenly left the other two and came over to Albert and said, 'Excuse me, I am the manager of the English team. The Duke has sent a message to say that he is held up by a traffic block and he wants us to carry on without him. Would you care to kick off for us?'

Albert's mouth fell open. No words would come.

Then he felt Angus nudging him and saying, 'Of course he will kick off for you. He'll be very glad to – won't you, Albert?' Now Angus was pushing him out of his seat and into the gangway. 'And I'll come with him,' he added.

And Albert was out on the pitch, with his mouth still open and Angus by his side, chatting happily with the manager.

Albert managed to close his mouth again while he was introduced to the Scottish team and Angus was introduced to the English team, but it was not until he was set in front of the ball that he gasped out, 'I've never kicked a ball!'

'Never mind,' answered the manager, 'all we need is for you to get the ball into play.'

Albert went back a few paces and ran forward, kicking the ball so well that everybody gasped with amazement, except Albert, who was flat on his back and could not see where the ball had gone.

With a wild, highland whoop, Angus was off after the

ball, but the manager, who had introduced himself as Mr Calder, grabbed him and pointed out that now they must get out of the way of the players. Angus was disappointed, but he helped heave the still dazed Albert to his feet and they ran to the side of the pitch.

'Now,' said Mr Calder, 'it's only right that you should both come and sit in the directors' box.'

This time it was Angus who was flabbergasted, but he soon recovered, and the two bears followed Mr Calder up the steps and into the comfortable chairs of the big open box.

Two minutes later, all three of them were yelling their heads off and Albert was madly waving his rattle encouraging their own teams to score.

At half-time there had been no score and everyone enjoyed the drinks that were passed round to ease throats hoarse with shouting.

Suddenly the manager prodded Angus and Albert and said, 'Here he is, at last.'

'Who?'

'The Duke.'

'Here!'

'Of course. Come and be introduced.'

Clutching checked cap and tam o'shanter, they were introduced to the Duke who actually *thanked* them for helping him.

'Not at all, we were very pleased to do it,' Albert managed to gasp out.

Although he was shouting and waving his rattle for the English team, Albert was secretly rather pleased when the Scottish team won by two goals to one. After saying a very contented goodbye and thank you all round, the two bears went home by the tube train again, but Angus was too full of the match to want to do any extra riding on the moving stair.

Albert stirred up the fire and put on some coal and then he prepared a big tea, for they were very hungry. It was while they were buttering their second oatcake and Albert was passing the last pot of Extra Rich honey that Angus said, 'Why don't you come up to Stirling next week for the Highland Games?'

'Could I?'

'Yes, of course. You'd like it very much. Caber tossing and putting the shot and wrestling and all the Scottish dancing. Will you come?'

'I certainly will. It is quite a while since I had a holiday, and I haven't seen Aunt Bertha for such a long time.'

They talked of the things they would do together in Scotland and then it was time to leave for the station. King's Cross was packed with happy, shouting Scots going home after winning the match. Angus found a seat and Albert stayed with him until the long train pulled out of the great station and he waved till it was out of sight.

As he went contentedly home, Albert thought about his coming visit to Stirling. 'I might buy myself a kilt,' he said.

from ALBERT

HONEY BEAR

by Elizabeth Lang

There was a big bear
Who lived in a cave;
His greatest love
Was honey.
He had twopence a week
Which he never could save,
So he never had
Any money.
I bought him a money box
Red and round,
In which to put
His money.
He saved and saved
Till he got a pound
Then he spent it all
On honey.

from THE BOOK OF A THOUSAND POEMS

HOW THE POLAR BEAR BECAME

by Ted Hughes

When the animals had been on earth for some time they grew tired of admiring the trees, the flowers, and the sun. They began to admire each other. Every animal was eager to be admired, and spent a part of each day making itself look more beautiful.

Soon they began to hold beauty contests.

Sometimes Tiger won the prize, sometimes Eagle, and sometimes Ladybird. Every animal tried hard.

One animal in particular won the prize almost every time. This was Polar Bear.

Polar Bear was white. Not quite snowy white, but much

whiter than any of the other creatures. Everyone admired her. In secret, too, everyone was envious of her. But however much they wished that she wasn't quite so beautiful, they couldn't help giving her the prize.

'Polar Bear,' they said, 'with your white fur, you are almost too beautiful.'

All this went to Polar Bear's head. In fact, she became vain. She was always washing and polishing her fur, trying to make it still whiter. After a while she was winning the prize every time. The only times any other creature got a chance to win was when it rained. On those days Polar Bear would say:

'I shall not go out in the wet. The other creatures will be muddy, and my white fur may get splashed.'

Then, perhaps, Frog or Duck would win for a change.

She had a crowd of young admirers who were always hanging around her cave. They were mainly Seals, all very giddy. Whenever she came out they made a loud shrieking roar:

'Ooooooh! How beautiful she is!'

Before long, her white fur was more important to Polar Bear than anything. Whenever a single speck of dust landed on the tip of one hair of it – she was furious.

'How can I be expected to keep beautiful in this country!' she cried then. 'None of you have ever seen me at my best, because of the dirt here. I am really much whiter than any of you have ever seen me. I think I shall have to go into another country. A country where there is none of this dust. Which country would be best?'

She used to talk in this way because then the Seals would cry:

'Oh, please don't leave us. Please don't take your beauty away from us. We will do anything for you.'

And she loved to hear this.

Soon animals were coming from all over the world to look

at her. They stared and stared as Polar Bear stretched out on her rock in the sun. Then they went off home and tried to make themselves look like her. But it was no use. They were all the wrong colour. They were black, or brown, or yellow, or ginger, or fawn, or speckled, but not one of them was white. Soon most of them gave up trying to look beautiful. But they still came every day to gaze enviously at Polar Bear. Some brought picnics. They sat in a vast crowd among the trees in front of her cave.

'Just look at her,' said Mother Hippo to her children. 'Now see that you grow up like that.'

But nothing pleased Polar Bear.

'The dust these crowds raise!' she sighed. 'Why can't I ever get away from them? If only there were some spotless, shining country, all for me . . . .'

Now pretty well all the creatures were tired of her being so much more admired than they were. But one creature more so than the rest. He was Peregrine Falcon.

He was a beautiful bird, all right. But he was not white. Time and again, in the beauty contests he was runner-up to Polar Bear.

'If it were not for her,' he raged to himself, 'I should be first every time.'

He thought and thought for a plan to get rid of her. How? How? How? At last he had it.

One day he went up to Polar Bear.

Now Peregrine Falcon had been to every country in the world. He was a great traveller, as all the creatures well knew.

'I know a country,' he said to Polar Bear, 'which is so clean it is even whiter than you are. Yes, yes, I know, you are beautifully white, but this country is even whiter. The rocks are clean glass and the earth is frozen ice-cream. There is no dirt there, no dust, no mud. You would become whiter than ever in that country. And no one lives there. You could be queen of it.'

Polar Bear tried to hide her excitement.

'I could be queen of it, you say?' she cried. 'This country sounds made for me. No crowds, no dirt? And the rocks, you say, are glass?'

'The rocks,' said Peregrine Falcon, 'are mirrors.'

'Wonderful!' cried Polar Bear.

'And the rain,' he said, 'is white face powder.'

'Better than ever!' she cried. 'How quickly can I be there, away from all these staring crowds and all this dirt?'

'I am going to another country,' she told the other animals. 'It is too dirty here to live.'

Peregrine Falcon hired Whale to carry his passenger. He sat on Whale's forehead, calling out the directions. Polar Bear sat on the shoulder, gazing at the sea. The Seals, who had begged to go with her, sat on the tail.

After some days, they came to the North Pole, where it is all snow and ice.

'Here you are,' cried Peregrine Falcon. 'Everything just as I said. No crowds, no dirt, nothing but beautiful clean whiteness.'

'And the rocks actually are mirrors!' cried Polar Bear, and she ran to the nearest iceberg to repair her beauty after the long trip.

Every day now, she sat on one iceberg or another, making herself beautiful in the mirror of the ice. Always, near her, sat the Seals. Her fur became whiter and whiter in this new clean country. And as it became whiter, the Seals praised her beauty more and more. When she herself saw the improvement in her looks she said:

'I shall never go back to that dirty old country again.'

And there she is still, with all her admirers around her.

Peregrine Falcon flew back to the other creatures and

told them that Polar Bear had gone for ever. They were all glad, and set about making themselves beautiful at once. Every single one was saying to himself:

'Now that Polar Bear is out of the way, perhaps I shall have a chance of the prize at the beauty contest.'

And Peregrine Falcon was saying to himself:

'Surely, now, I am the most beautiful of all creatures.'

But that first contest was won by Little Brown Mouse for her pink feet.

from HOW THE WHALE BECAME

WHY THE BEAR HAS NO TAIL

Once, a long time ago, a bear was sitting sunning himself and wondering what he could have to eat since he was beginning to feel hungry. Just then he noticed a fox who was hurrying past with a string of fish. Now the fox had most certainly stolen the fish from someone, for he was much too crafty to bother to fish for himself. But the bear did not realise this; all he could think of was how he was feeling hungrier and hungrier and how much he fancied a tasty piece of fish at that moment.

'Where did you get those fish?' he asked the fox.

Now the fox was very sly, and he thought that if he told the bear that he had stolen the fish, the bear might decide that he too could steal them from the fox and eat them himself. This was the more likely since the bear was considerably bigger and stronger than the fox. But the fox was far cleverer than the bear, so the fox thought of a way to distract the bear.

'I fished for them of course' lied the fox.

'Is that very difficult?' asked the bear. 'Could I catch some too?'

'Nothing easier' replied the fox. 'If you come with me I'll be glad to teach you.'

So the fox took the bear onto the ice and said 'All you have to do is make a hole in the ice. Then you lower your tail into the water and wait, and the longer you wait the more fish you will be able to catch. Don't worry if your tail hurts a little, since that's a sign that the fish are biting. If you follow my instructions, you'll soon find how easy it is to catch fish.'

The bear did exactly as the fox had told him and found that, sure enough, his tail started to nip a good deal, since it was soon frozen solid into the ice. But the bear sat there bravely, licking his lips gleefully as he thought of the large numbers of fish he was sure he was catching. When evening came he decided to collect his supper, but he had to tug so hard at his frozen tail to get it out of the ice, that his tail snapped off completely.

And that is why the bear has no tail to this day.

TRADITIONAL

THE POLAR BEAR

by Hilaire Belloc

The Polar Bear is unaware
    Of cold that cuts me through:
For why? He has a coat of hair.
    I wish I had one too!

from THE BAD CHILD'S BOOK OF BEASTS

TEDDY BEAR

by A. A. Milne

A bear, however hard he tries,
Grows tubby without exercise.
Our Teddy Bear is short and fat,
Which is not to be wondered at;
He gets what exercise he can
By falling off the ottoman,
But generally seems to lack
The energy to clamber back.

Now tubbiness is just the thing
Which gets a fellow wondering;
And Teddy worried lots about
The fact that he was rather stout.
He thought: 'If only I were thin!
But how does anyone begin?'
He thought: 'It really isn't fair
To grudge me exercise and air.'

For many weeks he pressed in vain
His nose against the window-pane,
And envied those who walked about
Reducing their unwanted stout.
None of the people he could see
'Is quite' (he said) 'as fat as me!'

Then, with a still more moving sigh,
'I mean' (he said) 'as fat as I!'

Now Teddy, as was only right,
Slept in the ottoman at night,
And with him crowded in as well
More animals than I can tell;
Not only these, but books and things,
Such as a kind relation brings –
Old tales of 'Once upon a time,'
And history retold in rhyme.

One night it happened that he took
A peep at an old picture-book,
Wherein he came across by chance
The picture of a King of France
(A stoutish man) and, down below,
These words: 'King Louis So and So,
Nicknamed "The Handsome!"' There he sat,
And (think of it!) the man was fat!

Our bear rejoiced like anything
To read about this famous King,
Nicknamed 'The Handsome.' There he sat,
And certainly the man was fat.
Nicknamed 'The Handsome.' Not a doubt
The man was definitely stout.
Why then, a bear (for all his tub)
Might yet be named 'The Handsome Cub!'

'Might yet be named.' Or did he mean
That years ago he 'might have been?'
For now he felt a slight misgiving:
'Is Louis So and So still living?
Fashions in beauty have a way
Of altering from day to day.
Is "Handsome Louis" with us yet?
Unfortunately I forget.'

Next morning (nose to window-pane)
The doubt occurred to him again.
One question hammered in his head:
'Is he alive or is he dead?'
Thus, nose to pane, he pondered; but
The lattice window, loosely shut,
Swung open. With one startled 'Oh!'
Our Teddy disappeared below.

There happened to be passing by
A plump man with a twinkling eye,
Who, seeing Teddy in the street,
Raised him politely to his feet,
And murmured kindly in his ear
Soft words of comfort and of cheer:
'Well, well!' 'Allow me!' 'Not at all.'
'Tut-tut! A very nasty fall.'

Our Teddy answered not a word;
It's doubtful if he even heard.
Our bear could only look and look:
The stout man in the picture-book!
That 'handsome' King – could this be he,
This man of adiposity?
'Impossible,' he thought. 'But still,
No harm in asking. Yes I will!'

'Are you,' he said, 'by any chance
His Majesty the King of France?'
The other answered, 'I am that,'
Bowed stiffly, and removed his hat;
Then said, 'Excuse me,' with an air,
'But is it Mr Edward Bear?'
And Teddy, bending very low,
Replied politely, 'Even so!'

They stood beneath the window there,
The King and Mr Edward Bear,
And, handsome, if a trifle fat,
Talked carelessly of this and that . . .
Then said His Majesty, 'Well, well,
I must get on,' and rang the bell.
'Your bear, I think,' he smiled. 'Good-day!'
And turned, and went upon his way.

A bear, however hard he tries,
Grows tubby without exercise.
Our Teddy Bear is short and fat,
Which is not to be wondered at.
But do you think it worries him
To know that he is far from slim?
No, just the other way about –
He's *proud* of being short and stout.

from WHEN WE WERE VERY YOUNG

WINNIE-THE-POOH GOES VISITING AND GETS INTO A TIGHT PLACE

by A. A. Milne

Edward Bear, known to his friends as Winnie-the-Pooh, or Pooh for short, was walking through the forest one day, humming proudly to himself. He had made up a little hum that very morning, as he was doing his Stoutness Exercises in front of the glass: *Tra-la-la, tra-la-la,* as he stretched up as high as he could go, and then *Tra-la-la, tra-la – oh, help! – la,* as he tried to reach his toes. After breakfast he had said it over and over to himself until he had learnt it off by heart, and now he was humming it right through, properly. It went like this:

> *Tra-la-la, tra-la-la,*
> *Tra-la-la, tra-la-la,*
> *Rum-tum-tiddle-um-tum.*
> *Tiddle-iddle, tiddle-iddle,*
> *Tiddle-iddle, tiddle-iddle,*
> *Rum-tum-tum-tiddle-um.*

Well, he was humming this hum to himself, and walking gaily along, wondering what everybody else was doing, and what it felt like, being somebody else, when suddenly he came to a sandy bank, and in the bank was a large hole.

'Aha!' said Pooh. *(Rum-tum-tiddle-um-tum.)* 'If I know anything about anything, that hole means Rabbit,' he said, 'and Rabbit means Company,' he said, 'and Company means Food and Listening-to-Me-Humming and such like. *Rum-tum-tum-tiddle-um.*'

So he bent down, put his head into the hole, and called out:

'Is anybody at home?'

There was a sudden scuffling noise from inside the hole, and then silence.

'What I said was, "Is anybody at home?"' called out Pooh very loudly.

'No!' said a voice; and then added, 'You needn't shout so loud. I heard you quite well the first time.'

'Bother!' said Pooh. 'Isn't there anybody here at all?'

'Nobody.'

Winnie-the-Pooh took his head out of the hole, and thought for a little, and he thought to himself, 'There must be somebody there, because somebody must have *said* "Nobody."' So he put his head back in the hole, and said:

'Hallo, Rabbit, isn't that you?'

'No,' said Rabbit, in a different sort of voice this time.

'But isn't that Rabbit's voice?'

'I don't *think* so,' said Rabbit. 'It isn't *meant* to be.'

'Oh!' said Pooh.

He took his head out of the hole, and had another think, and then he put it back, and said:

'Well, could you very kindly tell me where Rabbit is?'

'He has gone to see his friend Pooh Bear, who is a great friend of his.'

'But this *is* Me!' said Bear, very much surprised.

'What sort of Me?'

'Pooh Bear.'

'Are your sure?' said Rabbit, still more surprised.

'Quite, quite sure,' said Pooh.

'Oh, well, then, come in.'

So Pooh pushed and pushed and pushed his way through the hole, and at last he got in.

'You were quite right,' said Rabbit, looking at him all over. 'It *is* you. Glad to see you.'

'Who did you think it was?'

'Well, I wasn't sure. You know how it is in the Forest. One can't have *anybody* coming into one's house. One has to be *careful*. What about a mouthful of something?'

Pooh always liked a little something at eleven o'clock in the morning, and he was very glad to see Rabbit getting out the plates and mugs; and when Rabbit said, 'Honey or condensed milk with your bread?' he was so excited that he said, 'Both,' and then, so as not to seem greedy, he added, 'But don't bother about the bread, please.' And for a long time after that he said nothing . . . until at last, humming to himself in a rather sticky voice, he got up, shook Rabbit lovingly by the paw, and said that he must be going on.

'Must you?' said Rabbit politely.

'Well,' said Pooh, 'I could stay a little longer if it – if you —' and he tried very hard to look in the direction of the larder.

'As a matter of fact,' said Rabbit, 'I was going out myself directly.'

'Oh well, then, I'll be going on. Good-bye.'

'Well, good-bye, if you're sure you won't have any more.'

'*Is* there any more?' asked Pooh quickly.

Rabbit took the covers off the dishes, and said, 'No, there wasn't.'

'I thought not,' said Pooh, nodding to himself. 'Well, good-bye. I must be going on.'

So he started to climb out of the hole. He pulled with his front paws, and pushed with his back paws, and in a little while his nose was out in the open again . . . and then his ears . . . and then his front paws . . . and then his shoulders . . . and then——

'Oh, help!' said Pooh. 'I'd better go back.'

'Oh, bother!' said Pooh. 'I shall have to go on.'

'I can't do either!' said Pooh. 'Oh, help *and* bother!'

Now, by this time Rabbit wanted to go for a walk too, and finding the front door full, he went out by the back door, and came round to Pooh, and looked at him.

'Hallo, are you stuck?' he asked.

'N-no,' said Pooh carelessly. 'Just resting and thinking

and humming to myself.'

'Here, give us a paw.'

Pooh Bear stretched out a paw, and Rabbit pulled and pulled and pulled. . . .

'*Ow!*' cried Pooh. 'You're hurting!'

'The fact is,' said Rabbit, 'you're stuck.'

'It all comes,' said Pooh crossly, 'of not having front doors big enough.'

'It all comes,' said Rabbit sternly, 'of eating too much. I thought at the time,' said Rabbit, 'only I didn't like to say anything,' said Rabbit, 'that one of us was eating too much,' said Rabbit, 'and I knew it wasn't *me*,' he said. 'Well, well, I shall go and fetch Christopher Robin.'

Christopher Robin lived at the other end of the Forest, and when he came back with Rabbit, and saw the front half of Pooh, he said, 'Silly old Bear,' in such a loving voice that everybody felt quite hopeful again.

'I was just beginning to think,' said Bear, sniffing slightly, 'that Rabbit might never be able to use his front door again. And I should *hate* that,' he said.

'So should I,' said Rabbit.

'Use his front door again?' said Christopher Robin. 'Of course he'll use his front door again.'

'Good,' said Rabbit.

'If we can't pull you out, Pooh, we might push you back.'

Rabbit scratched his whiskers thoughtfully, and pointed out that, when once Pooh was pushed back, he was back, and of course nobody was more glad to see Pooh than *he* was, still there it was, some lived in trees and some lived underground, and——

'You mean I'd *never* get out?' said Pooh.

'I mean,' said Rabbit, 'that having got *so* far, it seems a pity to waste it.'

Christopher Robin nodded.

'Then there's only one thing to be done,' he said. 'We

shall have to wait for you to get thin again.'

'How long does getting thin take?' asked Pooh anxiously.

'About a week, I should think.'

'But I can't stay here for a *week!*'

'You can *stay* here all right, silly old Bear. It's getting you out which is so difficult.'

'We'll read to you,' said Rabbit cheerfully.

'And I hope it won't snow,' he added. 'And I say, old fellow, you're taking up a good deal of room in my house – *do* you mind if I use your back legs as a towel-horse? Because, I mean, there they are – doing nothing – and it would be very convenient just to hang the towels on them.'

'A week!' said Pooh gloomily. *'What about meals?'*

'I'm afraid no meals,' said Christopher Robin, 'because of getting thin quicker. But we *will* read to you.'

Bear began to sigh, and then found he couldn't because he was so tightly stuck; and a tear rolled down his eye, as he said:

'Then would you read a Sustaining Book, such as would help and comfort a Wedged Bear in Great Tightness?'

So for a week Christopher Robin read that sort of book at the North end of Pooh, and Rabbit hung his washing on the South end . . . and in between Bear felt himself getting slenderer and slenderer. And at the end of the week Christopher Robin said, *'Now!'*

So he took hold of Pooh's front paws and Rabbit took hold of Christopher Robin, and all Rabbit's friends and relations took hold of Rabbit, and they all pulled together . . .

And for a long time Pooh only said *'Ow!'* . . .

And *'Oh!'* . . .

And then, all of a sudden, he said *'Pop!'* just as if a cork were coming out of a bottle.

And Christopher Robin and Rabbit and all Rabbit's friends and relations went head-over-heels backwards . . . and on the top of them came Winnie-the-Pooh – free!

So, with a nod of thanks to his friends, he went on with his walk through the forest, humming proudly to himself. But, Christopher Robin looked after him lovingly, and said to himself, 'Silly old Bear!'

from WINNIE-THE-POOH

PADDINGTON'S
VISIT TO THE CINEMA

by Michael Bond

*Paddington is a small bear who somehow causes chaos wherever he
goes, though he always means well. He has become a permanent
member of the Brown family – Mr and Mrs Brown, Judy, Jonathan
and their housekeeper Mrs Bird – ever since they first found him,
wandering forlornly on Paddington Station.*

'I'm afraid,' said the lady in the cash desk at the Podium
Super Cinema, 'you can't come in. It's an "A" film.'

'I beg your pardon?' said Paddington, looking puzzled.

'"A",' said the lady.

'Eh?' repeated Paddington, looking even more puzzled.

'But that's what I said.'

'Not "eh",' said the lady impatiently. '"A". That means bears under sixteen aren't allowed in unaccompanied.'

'Sixteen!' exclaimed Paddington, hardly able to believe his ears. '*Sixteen!* But I'm only two. That's another fourteen years. I might not even want to come then.'

'Well, that's the law,' said the lady sternly. She looked down with some distaste at the top of Paddington's hat. It still had one or two pieces of river weed sticking to it and the warmth of the cinema was bringing out the smell. 'Now come along, please,' she said hastily. 'You're holding up the queue.'

'And no coming back later on wearing long trousers,' she called as Paddington turned to go. 'I know all the tricks.'

Paddington felt most disappointed as he made his way slowly across the foyer. There was a nice warm feeling about the cinema and he particularly liked the way his feet sank into the thick pile of the carpet. After staring hungrily at the sweet counter for a few moments he made his way towards the entrance, giving the attendant a hard stare as the man held the door open for him.

Paddington had never been to the pictures before. In fact he wasn't at all sure what they were. But he enjoyed anything new and for some weeks he had been saving hard out of the six pence a week bun money Mr Brown gave him, in case an interesting programme came along.

Paddington was a bear who liked getting his money's worth and he'd carefully studied the advertisements outside the Podium until this week, when there was a 'Super Double Feature' programme showing – with two long films, a cartoon and a newsreel. Not only that, but a notice outside said there was a special added attraction that evening when Reginald Clove would be playing the theatre organ during the intervals.

Paddington hung about outside the cinema for several

minutes breathing heavily on the glass until he caught sight of a policeman watching him suspiciously and then he hurried home. It was all most disappointing and his carefully saved nine pence was burning a hole in his duffle coat pocket.

'Do you mean to say you've never been to the pictures, Paddington?' said Mr Brown over tea that afternoon.

'*Never*,' said Paddington firmly, as he helped himself to a crumpet. 'And now I can't go for another fourteen years unless I'm accompanied.'

Mr Brown looked at his wife. 'It's a long time since we all went to the pictures, Mary,' he said. 'And it's still quite early. Shall we go?'

'Gosh, Dad – let's!' exclaimed Jonathan and Judy together.

'Do you think it's a good programme, Paddington?' asked Mrs Brown.

'Very good, Mrs Brown,' said Paddington knowledgeably. 'There's a cowboy film and a cartoon and an "I beg your pardon film" as well.'

'A *what* film?' exclaimed Mr Brown.

'An "I beg your pardon film",' repeated Paddington. 'That means bears under sixteen aren't allowed in by themselves.'

'Oh, you mean an "A" film,' said Jonathan.

'That's right,' agreed Paddington. 'That's what I said.'

The Browns looked at one another. Sometimes it was a bit difficult explaining things to Paddington.

'*And* there's a man playing the organ,' continued Paddington. 'It's a special attraction – so I think it's a very good bargain, Mr Brown.'

'That settles it,' said Mr Brown, looking at his watch. 'It all sounds much too good to miss.'

Immediately the whole house was in an uproar. Paddington was sent upstairs by Mrs Bird to wash the crumpet stains off his whiskers while the rest of the family hurried off to their respective rooms to change.

Paddington felt very superior some half an hour later when they all trooped into the Podium Cinema. He raised his hat to the doorkeeper and then led Mr Brown in the direction of the cash desk.

'I'm accompanied now,' he called out to the lady in charge.

The lady stared at Mr Brown. 'I beg your pardon?' she exclaimed. She sniffed and gave him a very strange look. It was most odd but she could distinctly smell fish again.

'What did you say?' she repeated.

'Nothing,' said Mr Brown hastily. 'Er . . . I'd like three and three halves for the front row of the circle, please.'

'Hurry up, Dad,' called Jonathan. 'I think the other programme's nearly finished.'

Leaving the lady in the cash desk looking most upset, Mr Brown gathered up a long string of tickets and joined the rest of the family as they hurried up the stairs leading to the circle.

They went up and up and Paddington soon lost count of the number of steps. In fact there were so many he almost wished they had gone downstairs instead. Not only that, but as he followed the Browns through the entrance to the circle he discovered it was all dark inside.

'This way, please,' said the usherette, as she led the way down some stairs and shone her torch along a row of seats in the front row. 'You're lucky. There are just six left together.'

'Thank you very much,' said Mrs Brown, as she made her way along the row. 'Excuse me, please. Excuse me. Thank you very much.'

She sat down and arranged herself comfortably as the others joined her.

'That's a bit of luck,' whispered Mr Brown. 'Finding six together.'

'Seven,' said Mrs Brown. 'There's still another one between us.'

'So there is!' whispered Mr Brown, groping in the dark. 'That's odd. The girl said there were only six.' He looked along the row. 'Where's Paddington?'

'Paddington?' exclaimed Mrs Brown. 'Isn't he with you, Henry?'

'No,' replied Mr Brown. 'I thought *you* had him.'

'Oh, crumbs,' groaned Judy. 'Trust Paddington to get lost.'

'Where on earth can he have got to?' grumbled Mr Brown as he struck a match and began looking under the seats.

'Here I am, Mr Brown,' called Paddington from the end of the row. 'I went all the way along by mistake.'

'Sssh!' said a nasty sounding voice from the row behind.

'It's all dark and I can't see,' exclaimed Paddington as he was passed back along the row.

'Are you all right now, dear?' whispered Mrs Brown, as Paddington sat down beside her.

'I think so,' said Paddington, peering at the screen.

'Oi!' said the nasty voice from behind again. ''Ow about taking yer titfer off?'

Paddington turned and stared in the direction of the speaker. 'My titfer?' he exclaimed. 'Take my *titfer* off?'

'That's right,' said the voice. 'Your tit for tat.'

'I think he means your hat, dear,' explained Mrs Brown. 'It's probably getting in the way of the screen.'

Paddington thought for a moment. He wasn't at all keen on taking his hat off in case it got lost in the dark. 'I'll turn it round if you like,' he said generously. 'Then you can look through one of the holes.'

Having solved the problem of the man behind, Paddington gave his attention to the screen. It was all very interesting, with people dashing about all over the place and with music that got louder and louder, but Paddington found it difficult to understand what it was all about. To his surprise, after only a few minutes the music suddenly ended and all the lights in the cinema came on.

'Well,' he exclaimed, looking most disappointed. 'I didn't think much of that!'

'It's all right, Paddington,' explained Judy. 'That's what's showing *next* week. That was only the trailer.'

But her words fell on empty ears for Paddington was staring at the screen again and licking his whiskers.

'Oh, dear,' groaned Mr Brown, as he followed Paddington's gaze. 'They *would* have to advertise ice-cream. They must have known he was coming.' He felt in his pocket. 'You'd better get six tubs, and some nougat or something for the big picture, Jonathan.'

'I think I'm going to enjoy myself,' announced Paddington a few minutes later as Mr Brown handed him the refreshments.

He dipped his spoon into the ice-cream tub and stared excitedly at the screen as the lights went down again to herald the start of the cowboy film.

Paddington enjoyed the cowboy film much more than the trailer, and he soon became quite lost in the story. He stood up on his seat with his paws on the balcony and his eyes glued on the screen. Every now and then he automatically dipped his spoon into the ice-cream tub and several times a lump fell off the spoon before it had even reached his mouth, which was most unusual.

It was all very complicated at first. Everyone seemed to be shooting at everyone else and Paddington got worried in case there was no one left and they had to stop the film.

Each time the villain, who wore a black mask and a black hat, came on to the screen he booed, and when the hero appeared, riding a white horse, he cheered and waved his hat in the air until Mrs Brown became quite embarrassed.

She wasn't at all sorry when at long last the hero rode off into the setting sun and the film came to an end.

'Most enjoyable,' said Mrs Bird, rather surprisingly. The Browns had somehow never thought of Mrs Bird liking cowboy films. 'Did you like it, Paddington?'

Paddington nodded his head vigorously. 'I enjoyed it very much, thank you, Mrs Bird,' he said. 'Except I can't find my nougat anywhere.'

'Never mind, Paddington,' said Mr Brown, after they had all searched in vain for it. 'I'll buy you some more in a minute. *After* we've heard the organ.'

He sat back heavily in his seat and then turned to Paddington. 'If you watch,' he explained, 'you'll see it come up through the floor in a moment.'

'Come up through the floor, Mr Brown?' exclaimed Paddington. 'I don't think I've ever seen an organ come up through the floor before.'

'Oh, dear,' said Mrs Bird. 'And it doesn't look as if you're going to now. Look!'

She pointed to the screen where an announcement had just been flashed on to say that Mr Reginald Clove was indisposed.

'What!' cried Paddington hotly as the words sank in. 'Reginald Clove indisposed!'

'That means he's ill, dear,' explained Mrs Brown. 'So he won't be playing after all.'

'How very disappointing,' said Mr Brown. 'It's a long time since I heard an organ. I was really looking forward to it.'

While the rest of the Browns watched the advertisements on the screen Paddington sank back into his seat and listened to Mr Brown explaining what the organ would have looked like had it come up through the floor. Mr Brown liked organs and went on for a long time about it.

'Henry,' said Mrs Brown when he had finished. 'Where's Paddington?'

'Paddington?' exclaimed Mr Brown. 'Don't tell me he's disappeared *again*. He was here a moment ago.'

'I do hope he isn't long wherever he's got to,' said Mrs Brown. 'We shall never hear the last of it if he misses the start of the big picture.'

But Paddington was already almost out of sight. He was hurrying up the aisle and out through the door marked EXIT. There was a purposeful expression on his face, one which the Browns would have recognized at once had they been able to see him.

Paddington wasn't the only one with a purposeful expression on his face at that moment. As he hurried down the stairs on one side of the cinema the manager of the Podium strode up the stairs leading to the projection box on the other.

There was something unusual going on in his theatre and he intended finding out what it was. He prided himself that the Podium was normally a very well run cinema but on this particular evening things had gone wrong from the beginning.

First of all the lady in the cash desk – usually a most reliable person – had complained of a fishy smell and mysterious voices saying they were accompanied coming from underneath her counter. Then Reginald Clove had caught his hand in a swing door and had announced the fact that he couldn't play the organ. Something to do with his not being able to work the stops and turn the music with only one hand.

As if that wasn't enough there had come news of 'goings on' in the circle. It was most unusual to have 'goings on' in the circle. Occasionally he had a spot of bother in the cheaper seats downstairs – but never in the circle.

There had been complaints of bear's boos coming from the front row during the cowboy film, and as he'd passed through the stalls he'd also noticed several people immediately underneath the balcony with ice-cream stains on their hats. It was all very disturbing and he wasn't in the best of moods as he burst into the projection room waving a piece of paper.

'I want this notice flashed on the screen,' he said crossly. 'At once!'

'Good heavens!' exclaimed Mrs Brown a few moments later. 'What on earth can that mean?'

Mr Brown adjusted his glasses and stared at the screen. 'WILL THE OWNER OF THE YOUNG BEAR

IN THE CIRCLE KINDLY REPORT TO THE MANAGER'S OFFICE IMMEDIATELY,' he read.

'I don't know, Mary,' he said, as he made to get to his feet, 'but I'm certainly going to find out.'

'Owner indeed!' snorted Mrs Bird. 'As if anyone *owned* Paddington.'

'The boot's on the other paw, if you ask me,' began Mr Brown. 'Paddington owns *us*.' As he was speaking a strange expression came over his face.

'Well, Henry,' said Mrs Brown, staring at her husband, 'aren't you going to do something about it?'

'I . . . I can't get up,' exclaimed Mr Brown, feeling his seat. 'I seem to be stuck to something . . . Nougat!' he said bitterly. 'Paddington's nougat! No wonder the manager wants to see me in his office.'

Unaware of all the excitement that was going on, Paddington pushed open a door and made his way down the aisle of the stalls until he came across a girl selling ice-cream.

'Excuse me,' he said, climbing up on to a seat and tapping her on the shoulder, 'can you tell me where the indisposed man is?'

'The *indisposed* man?' repeated the girl.

'That's right,' said Paddington patiently. 'The one who's supposed to come up through the floor.'

'Oh, you mean the organist,' said the girl. 'Mr Reginald Clove. He's through that little door there. The one under the stage.'

Before she could explain that no one was allowed through it without permission Paddington had disappeared again.

Mr Reginald Clove looked quite startled when Paddington came through the door. He had been expecting *someone* to come, but he certainly hadn't expected it to be a bear.

'Are you from the first aid?' he asked, looking at Paddington rather doubtfully.

'Oh, no,' said Paddington, politely raising his hat. 'I'm from number thirty-two Windsor Gardens and I've come about the organ.'

Mr Clove stepped back a pace. 'You've come about the organ?' he repeated, trying to humour Paddington.

'Yes,' said Paddington. 'I wanted to see it come up through the floor.'

'Oh!' Mr Clove's face cleared. 'Is that all?'

'All!' exclaimed Paddington hotly. 'It's very important. Mr Brown was looking forward to it.'

'Oh, dear,' said Mr Clove, idly sorting through a pile of music with his good hand. 'I'm so sorry. I wish I could oblige. But I've hurt my hand, you see, and I've no one to turn the music for me, and . . .' He looked thoughtfully at Paddington. 'Do *you* like music, bear?' he asked suddenly.

'Oh, yes,' replied Paddington. 'But I don't really play anything except the comb and paper and I'm not very good at that because I get my whiskers caught in the comb.'

'Do you think you could turn the music for me?' asked Mr Clove.

'Well,' said Paddington doubtfully, 'it's a bit difficult for bears because of their paws, but it you could tell me when to do it I could try.'

Mr Clove came to a decision. 'You'll do,' he said briskly. 'Come with me.'

'*Goings on!*' exclaimed Mrs Bird, waving her handbag at the manager. 'They weren't "goings on". He was only enjoying himself.'

'Bear's boos,' said the manager sternly. 'In the Podium circle. And nougat on one of my best seats.'

'Then you shouldn't sell it,' replied Mrs Bird. 'It's asking for trouble.'

'Well, where is he now?' demanded the manager. 'Tell

me that. I want to start the big picture. We're five minutes late already.'

The Browns exchanged anxious glances. Knowing Paddington he might be anywhere, but before they had time to reply they were all startled into silence by a loud rumbling from the front of the cinema which grew and grew in volume until the whole place began to shake.

'Good heavens!' exclaimed the manager as a burst of applause swept through the audience. 'It's Reginald Clove playing "Rule Britannia!" And with one hand, too!'

They all stared over the balcony as the lights dimmed and the organ rose into view bathed in a pink spotlight.

'Mercy me,' cried Mrs Bird, clutching her seat. 'And there's that bear – what on earth is he doing now?'

Paddington felt most important as he rode up on the organ and he wished he could turn and wave to the Browns to let them know where he was, but he was much too busy carrying out Mr Clove's instructions.

Even so, there was one nasty moment when, in his excitement, he turned over two pages of music at once by mistake. Mr Clove looked most surprised when he suddenly found himself playing a selection from *The Gondoliers* instead of 'Rule Britannia', but he quickly recovered and in the general excitement no one seemed to notice.

The audience applauded all the items and Paddington felt quite sorry when Mr Clove at last pressed a button by his side and the organ began to sink back through the floor. But as it finally disappeared from view and the last notes of the music died away a loud cheer went up from the audience and several voices were heard shouting for more.

Afterwards everyone agreed that good though the big picture was, the organ had been the high spot of the evening. Even the manager of the Podium seemed very pleased and he took the Browns on a tour behind the scenes before they left.

'I don't suppose,' said Paddington thoughtfully, as they made their way home, 'there are many bears who've been for a ride on an organ. Especially one that comes up through the floor.'

'And I don't suppose,' said Mr Brown, as he turned and looked hard at Paddington, 'that there are many people who've been stuck to their seat by a piece of bear's nougat.'

But Paddington had his eyes closed. He wasn't exactly asleep, but he had a lot of things to write in his scrap-book that night when he went to bed. He'd enjoyed his visit to the pictures and it needed a lot of careful thought to put it all into words.

from PADDINGTON HELPS OUT

MARY PLAIN
AND ST BRUIN'S DAY

by Gwynedd Rae

Mary Plain is a little bear who lives in a zoo in Switzerland with the other bears in her family. Her aunt Friska looks after Mary and her little cousins are called Marionetta and Little Wool.

The GREAT DAY had come at last. After breakfast Mary's grandmother, Big Wool, stood up and cleared her throat and said, in a very serious way –

'Bears! This is St Bruin's Day, and I hope we all realise, *all* realise – Mary,' she said, for Mary didn't seem to be listening quite attentively, 'how great an occasion this is. We shall take very special care with our toilet this morning, and at six we shall meet again to have a final brush up.' (Mary sighed loudly.) 'In the meantime, I ask you all to pass the day in a fitting manner.' She was so pleased with the last sentence, that she gave a little cough, and repeated, 'in a fitting manner.' 'I think that is all I have to say – except that, when we all meet this evening before waiting on our – on our – ancestors,' said Big Wool, getting a little muddled, 'you will, of course, all bring with you the slight offerings you have put aside.'

This brought Mary to full attention. Gracious Heavens! She hadn't got an offering. Last night she'd had one – a beautiful pink juicy carrot with the leaves still on – how juicy it had been she was, alas, in a position to know only too well – for, to stop a queer 'asking' feeling in her waist, she had eaten that carrot in the small hours of the morning.

Only now did she realize what a terrible thing she had done. There wasn't the slightest hope of getting another such carrot. It was the biggest she'd even seen and it was pure luck that it had fallen to her share, so beautifully – just the day before St Bruin's Day, and she had been so proud and pleased and guarded it in a corner all day. Oh dear, oh dear, she must have been mad, and indeed she had been half asleep.

She collected frantically all the morning and at midday retired to a corner and examined her store.

One faded carrot stalk, two very small figs, half a biscuit, and an empty milk tin; oh – and a cork.

She sat down and eyed them sadly. She was quite certain the carrot stalk and the figs wouldn't do and she felt sure that neither Alpha nor Lady Grizzle, her great-grandparents, would appreciate half a biscuit, especially as she knew for a fact that Marionetta had a whole one she'd saved from last week. No! It was between the tin and the cork. Suddenly she pounced on the tin – a hole in it! If the cork would fit! Her paws shook with excitement as she tried to persuade the cork into a hole half as big as itself – but presently she threw both away in disgust.

Then she thought of developing a frightfully sudden cold, so she went and stood just under the wall which divided the Nursery from Parlour Pit, and sneezed for ten minutes. But, alas, they can't have been very good imitations for she distinctly heard Big Wool say to Friska, 'Listen to those cubs. They must be playing at doctors, for one of them is pretending to have a cold.' So that was no good.

Just then, a strange kind of whistle made her look up at the railings above. At that very moment she saw a little boy there open his mouth to speak, and out dropped something which fell into the pit, close to Mary. He seemed most upset at having lost it and wanted to climb over to fetch it, but his mother didn't seem to want him to do this. Mary thought to herself, 'If he's so unhappy at losing it, it must be something rather important – perhaps a tooth,' and she picked it up and had a look. It wasn't a tooth at all. It was round and small and shiny, like silver, and had a hole in the middle, but, though she licked it, it didn't have any taste. However she'd decided it must be a kind of sweet, for the boy had it in his mouth. At any rate, that settled it. She'd take it to the two old bears, and if they didn't like it she couldn't help it – it was the best she could do, and at least it was shiny. So she went and hid it under a loose stone in the corner of the pit, to keep it quite safe till the evening.

'What *are* you going to do about your present?' asked the twins, later on, for Mary had told them about the carrot. 'Won't you be very frightened to go without anything?'

'But I've got something,' said Mary casually.

'Oh, what?'

'Something, I said.'

'Oh, but do tell us what.'

'No, it's a secret,' and she kept it all day.

As soon as the doors were up, all the business of getting tidy had to be gone through again, and Mary was heartily sick of it, and very thankful St Bruin's Day only came once a year. At the end they all stood up and recited the poem they had been learning in school all that week, to be sure they had it quite right. It went like this:

> '*Many happy years we wish to you,*
> *May carrots and dried figs your pit-floor strew,*
> *We hope that happiness will with you stay*
> *Till we all meet on next St Bruin's Day.*
>
> *By Friska*'

'Be sure not to forget to say "by Friska," will you?' said Friska anxiously – she was so very proud of having written the poem – and they all promised to remember.

Then Mary slipped off and flew to the corner where she had hidden her present. She felt quite anxious as she lifted the stone, in case anyone had stolen it, but it was still there safe and sound and she breathed a sigh of relief and popped it into her mouth. That was where the small boy had kept it, so obviously it was the safest plan to do the same. She was so quick that no one had noticed her absence, and she got back just in time to hear Big Wool say, 'Now, are we all ready? And don't forget to bow!' And it began to be rather exciting.

Mary felt her heart going pit-a-pat and she stood up very straight and tried to turn her feet out. Unfortunately Little Wool spoke to her just as she was stepping over the doorstep into Den Pit, and she caught her paw and fell in flat on her face. However, Friska, who was in front, picked her up quickly and smoothed her down, so no real damage was done.

It is true she had *very* nearly swallowed her present, but, as she had not *quite* done so, it did not matter.

Now the cubs had heard these two old bears talked about a great deal and they had been told they were very wonderful and wise and knew everything there was to know, and as they had heard all this and yet had never seen them they seemed all the more mysterious. When Mary's turn came she was determined to make a very good impression.

Alpha was sitting on the edge of the bath to receive them and Lady Grizzle stood just beside him.

'You now,' said Friska, who was standing at the side and telling them each when their turn came.

Mary stepped forward and made a really beautiful bow. Then she took a deep breath, opened her mouth and out came, not the expected poem, but a piercing whistle. Mary looked very surprised and so did all the others, and they looked round to see if anyone else had come into the pit. But no one had, so Mary tried again and the same thing happened, so then she knew it must be herself. This time, however, she was determined to get through the poem, so she went on, whistling bravely till Friska, who saw Alpha was getting angry, came and pulled her away. She whispered to Bunch to go and say the poem again, and to go on saying it till she told him to stop, so as to keep Alpha busy. Then she led Mary into the farthest corner and said, 'Don't you feel very well, Mary?'

'Wheee –' whistled Mary.

Friska started. This was serious. She had heard of people losing their voices during a bad cold, but never of their making a noise like this, and besides, Mary had not had a cold. She put her arm round her and said kindly, 'Tell Auntie where it hurts, Mary dear?'

'Wheee –' went Mary.

Every time she made this extraordinary sound, Friska looked anxiously to see if Alpha had heard, but Bunch was saying the poem in such a loud voice, that she did not think he could have.

'There, there, there,' she said soothingly. 'I'm sure it will soon be better,' and she rubbed Mary's tummy gently. But Mary shook her head violently and pushed her paw away. 'Wheee – Wheee – Wheee –!' she whistled earnestly.

Friska said, 'Sch' again, and then looked at her helplessly. It was so like Mary to go and get unwell on this most important day, and such an odd kind of illness, too. She might at least have chosen a silent one, or one that could be understood and cured like a sore throat or a tummy-ache.

Just then Big Wool hurried up and Friska drew her on one side and explained. 'I know,' said Big Wool, capably, 'a firm hand. Leave her to me!' and she nodded her head knowingly. Then she came to Mary, clapped her paws sharply, and said, 'Come, come, Mary, enough of this nonsense! Just stop making that noise and behave yourself. I can't imagine what you –' 'Wheee –' interrupted Mary. Big Wool stood and blinked and then she turned Mary slowly round, while she felt her carefully all over. But she could not find anything wrong.

Now Mary was getting rather tired of all this fussing, so she decided she would go and give Alpha his present and give up trying to say the poem again, and she started off towards him. Directly Big Wool and Friska saw where she was going they rushed after her and each taking a paw they led her firmly back into the corner. 'Wheee –!' said Mary, trying to explain, but Friska put her paw over her mouth and said, 'Sch! Sch! Quiet, Mary, quiet.' And Big Wool stroked her in long soothing strokes down her back, which Mary hated, but she could not speak, so she had to bear it.

'Shall we take her home?' suggested Big Wool, but at this Mary whistled so loud and so long that it took them some moments to silence her. When she was quiet again, Friska beckoned to Big Wool and said in a low voice, 'Perhaps she'll take a sudden turn for the better?' But Big Wool shook her head. 'I doubt it, I doubt it,' she said, 'it looks to me very bad.'

While they were talking, Mary took the opportunity to escape again, and this time she got to within a few feet of Alpha before Friska caught her and dragged her back again.

'Oh dear, oh dear, what *can* we do?' she said to Big Wool. 'We can't go on like this. What do you suggest?'

Mary turned away and putting her paws behind her back, she kicked the ground a bit, to show she did not know they were talking about her.

'How about a slice of cake?' said Big Wool, and Friska trotted off briskly to fetch one. When she brought it back, Mary felt suddenly so terribly hungry that she forgot all about the little thing in her mouth and took a huge bite of cake. Then she choked and choked and they had to pat her on the back and finally shake her by the heels and, as they did this, out dropped something which fell with a tinkle on the ground and rolled away.

'Let me go, let me go,' shrieked Mary, kicking for all she was worth, and Big Wool was so surprised at hearing her speak again that she let go rather too quickly and Mary fell with a thud on to the floor. But she scrambled up, rushed to pick up the little disc, and before anyone could stop her, she had flown across the pit to Alpha's seat. Now Bunch was just saying the poem for the thirty-second time, in a rather hoarse voice, and Alpha was so sick of it, that he was almost glad of any interruption – even Mary.

She was a little out of breath when she reached him. 'Here is your present, and oh please take it because it's so little and I am afraid of losing it and I do hope you'll like it,' she said, all in a rush – and laid it on his knee.

Alpha looked at it. 'Is this a practical joke?' he asked sternly.

'Oh, no,' said Mary, 'it's a kind of noise and you keep it in your mouth.'

Alpha did not look as if he believed it, but he placed it in his mouth all the same, and sure enough out came a low whistle. He took it out hastily. 'Is that me, or is it still you making that noise?' he asked Mary suspiciously.

'No, sir, it was you,' said Mary.

Alpha looked again at the round thing in his paw, and putting it into his mouth he blew, and out came another splendid whistle. A slow, broad smile crept over his face, and he sat down and blew and whistled and whistled and blew for several minutes, looking more and more pleased.

Then he beckoned Mary to him and patting her on the shoulder said, 'Well, well, my cub, you have brought me a most interesting present, and I am very pleased, very pleased.'

So Mary's gift was the greatest success after all, and, when they went away that evening, they left Alpha sitting happily under the tree, blowing the whistle as loud as he could.

from MOSTLY MARY

TEDDY BEAR AND THE ALARM CLOCK

by Aaron Judah

Little Teddy Bear was excited about the picnic he was going to early the following morning. The other bears had asked him to come along with them. They were to meet at the railway station before the sun came up. They were planning an early start because the earlier they left the longer they would have in the country.

Teddy was *thrilled* at the idea of seeing the country again. The fun he would have running through the fields, paddling in the streams, eating honey sandwiches and drinking lemonade! The thought of it all made him clap his hands with delight.

His only trouble was getting up in the morning. He was a heavy sleeper, and as he lived all alone in a little bungalow he was afraid he might not wake up early enough. He had a wrist-watch, but that was no use. What he needed was a nice loud alarm clock to wake him, and fortunately his next-door neighbour, Mr Early Bird, had such a clock to lend him. Mr Bird kindly set the alarm to ring at five o'clock. He also wound it before he gave it to Teddy, and wished him a pleasant picnic.

'Are you sure it will ring on time?' asked Teddy anxiously. 'I've cut my sandwiches and packed them, and bought two bottles of fizzy lemonade. I don't want to wake up too late for the picnic.'

'Don't worry about my alarm clock,' said Mr Early Bird, confidently tapping him on the chest with one finger. It's served me faithfully the past ten years. Never let me down once. Just listen to it tick, my friend.'

Teddy put it to his ear. It went:

TICK TOCK TICK TOCK

Teddy had never heard such a loud tick in his life. It gave him confidence. He thanked Mr Early Bird for his alarm clock, and took it home with him. He packed his food and drink in a knapsack to be ready for the morning, and put out the clothes he was going to wear on the picnic. When it grew dark and night came he put the alarm clock on his bedside table, and switched off his bedside lamp. He thought to himself: I hope that no one will make any noise outside my window. I'll need all the sleep I can get to be fresh for the picnic. After all, I'm going to be woken by the alarm clock at five.

So saying, he at once shut his eyes, and imagined he was

falling asleep. As soon as he did this he began to hear something. It went:

TICK TOCK TICK TOCK

It's the clock, he thought. I'll get used to it if I shut my eyes tight and take no notice. But he *didn't* get used to it. The clock seemed to get louder and louder. It went:

TICK TOCK TICK TOCK

There was *no* getting used to it. Teddy rolled over and buried his ears in his pillow. But it made no difference. He knew he had to do something to make the tick quieter, and suddenly he had a brilliant idea. He took the clock and put it inside one of his thick socks, which lay on the floor by the side of his bed. Then he put the clock-in-the-sock into his left boot. Pleased with himself, he shut his eyes and listened. The tick was much quieter. It went:

TICK TOCK TICK TOCK

But he could still hear it. Never mind, he thought, by and by I'll get used to it. But he didn't. He tossed and turned, and tried to imagine he was falling asleep. And all the time the clock went:

TICK TOCK TICK TOCK

Eventually he got out of bed and put the clock-in-the-sock-in-the-boot into a suitcase, and shut it. Then he returned to bed. I'm sure I won't hear it now, he thought, I'm absolutely certain. He shut his eyes and listened. He *could* hear it. Yes, it was much fainter, but he could still hear it. It went:

TICK TOCK TICK TOCK

Yes, it's not loud enough to keep me awake, he thought.

But he was wrong. Even that faint sound stopped him from falling asleep. He got out of bed feeling rather angry, and put the clock-in-the-sock-in-the-boot-in-the-suitcase into a large leather trunk, and slammed it shut. But I'm not satisfied with that, he thought – it may be fainter still, but I expect when I get into bed I'll hear it. It'll probably go:

TICK TOCK TICK TOCK

He thought: while I'm out of bed I might as well do something about it. So he put the clock-in-the-sock-in-the-boot-in-the-suitcase-in-the-trunk into a cupboard, and locked it. Then he went to bed, and listened.

I expect I can *still* hear it, he thought in despair. But this time, although he listened with all his might, he couldn't hear anything. And by and by he fell into a sound sleep.

During the night no one made any noise outside his window. Teddy, snug in his little bed, slept peacefully on, and dreamed he was walking with his knapsack to catch the train. One o'clock came, two o'clock came, three o'clock, then four. Promptly at five o'clock the alarm of the clock-in-the-sock-in-the-boot-in-the-suitcase-the-trunk-in-the-cupboard went off with a mighty ringing. But so well had Teddy muffled the sound of the tick-tock that neither could the ringing of the alarm be heard. Teddy didn't hear it.

Outside, the sun with its red gold beams began to rise and light the town. And Teddy slept on. The birds began to chirp and sing. And Teddy slept on. A train hooted in the station: Whoo whoooooo! it went, and chuffed very impatiently. While Teddy slept on and on.

Then all of a sudden a loud voice began calling him outside his window. Teddy half awoke. The knocker on his door went: Bang bang bang! The door of his bungalow burst open, and Bruno, one of Teddy's friends, rushed in quite out of breath.

'Teddy! Teddy!' He shook him hard by the shoulder. 'Sleeping still? You'll be late for the picnic! The train is leaving in a minute!'

'What!' cried Teddy, awaking and rising with a shout. He leapt out of bed and began to throw on his clothes.

'Let me help you with your socks!' cried Bruno kneeling on the floor. 'Hurry! Here's one sock, where's the other?'

'In the boot!' cried Teddy.

'Here's one boot, where's the other?' cried Bruno.

'In the suitcase!'

'Where's the suitcase?'

'In the trunk!'

'Where's the trunk?'

'In the cupboard!'

'But why on earth –?' asked his friend astonished.

'Because of the tick-tock!'

'Because of the tick-tock? What tick-tock?'

'The tick-tock of the clock!'

'The tick-tock of the clock?'

'Yes, the tick-tock of the clock-in-the-sock!'

'The tick-tock of the sock-in-the-clock?' asked Bruno, whose head was spinning.

'No! No!' exclaimed Teddy. 'Listen carefully, or you'll never get it right. The tick-tock of the clock-in-the-sock-in-the-boot!'

'The tock-tick of the click-in-the-boot-in-the-sock?'

'No! No! The tick-tock of the clock-in-the-sock-in-the-boot-in-the-suitcase!'

'The click-clock of the sock-in-the-tock-in-the-suit-in-the-bootcase?'

'No! No! No!' shrieked Teddy, 'The tick-tock of the clock-in-the-sock-in-the— !'

'Stop! For goodness' sake, stop! We've no time to go through all *that* again!' cried Bruno. 'The train's leaving!' He grabbed his friend with one hand, his knapsack with the other, and shouted, 'You'll just have to come along with one boot!'

They rushed out of the house and bolted down the street toward the railway station. Having only one boot on didn't stop Teddy running as fast as ever. In half a minute they were at the station. Whoo whooooooo! went the train's whistle. Peep-peeeeeep! went the guard's whistle. Dashing across the stone floor of the station, Bruno's feet went: Clack! Clack! Clack! Clack! Clack! Clack! Teddy's feet went: Clack! Thump! Clack! Thump! Clack! Thump!

They went through the ticket collector's barrier just as the train was on the point of leaving. The other bears, all watching for them out of the carriage windows, raised a hearty cheer to see them come racing up. Panting and gasping, they were helped by willing hands into the carriage, and as the train started they flopped into their seats to recover their breaths. It was only when the train was well out of the station that the other bears noticed Teddy's left foot.

'Why, Teddy!' they cried. 'Where's your left boot?'

Teddy took a deep breath. 'Bruno', he said, 'you tell them'.

'Well,' began Bruno, scratching his head for a while, 'as far as I remember it goes something like this: The slick-sock of the hoot in the tootcase is in the boot-in-the-bunk-in-the-cupboard.'

'No, no,' said Teddy very patiently, 'the tick-tock of the clock-in-the-sock-in-the-boot-in-the-suitcase-in-the-trunk-in-the-cupboard'. And he explained to them from the very beginning how he came to borrow Mr Early Bird's alarm clock, and all that he did to muffle its loud tick-tock.

They chuckled and had a good laugh over it. Bruno said, 'That's all very well laughing, Teddy, but how are you going to wake up early the next time we have a picnic?'

'I don't know,' said Teddy. 'It's a problem.'

'I shall just have to come and fetch you,' his friend said.

'We'll all come to fetch you, Teddy,' the other bears promised.

By and by the train stopped at their station, and they all tumbled helter skelter out of the carriage. In a few minutes they were out in the country, where they had a lovely day picnicing in the woods. Teddy had as good a time as any of them, because a missing boot can't bother a little bear very much when he's out on a picnic.

from TALES OF TEDDY BEAR

TEDDY ROBINSON
AND THE CHINA GNOME

by Joan G. Robinson

Teddy Robinson is a nice, big, comfortable, friendly teddy bear.
He has light brown fur and belongs to a little girl called Deborah.

One day Teddy Robinson and Deborah were looking at the marigolds and radishes coming up in their garden when the postman came by with a big parcel for Deborah. On one side it had a label which said FRAGILE. HANDLE WITH CARE.

'Now, what can that be?' said Deborah, and she ran indoors with it and sat Teddy Robinson down on the table so that he could watch while she opened it.

'Fragile. Handle with care,' said Deborah. 'I wonder what it is.'

'It's got a beautiful name,' said Teddy Robinson. 'I wish my name was fragile, but of course I haven't got a handle.'

'No, it isn't a name,' said Deborah, 'and it doesn't mean

it's got a handle. It means it's precious and mustn't be dropped or kicked around in case it gets broken.'

'Ah,' said Teddy Robinson, and he began singing:

> *'Fragile, fragile*
> *Teddy R.,*
> *what a precious bear I are.*
> *Never leave me on the ground*
> *in case I'm squashed or kicked around.*
> *Fragile, fragile –'*

'Don't be silly,' said Deborah, 'you aren't fragile. I expect this is some kind of ornament, that's what.'

'Well, I shall be called Fragile too,' said Teddy Robinson. 'I shall have it for my second name.'

Deborah pulled off the brown paper and opened the box, and there inside, among a lot of straw shavings, she found a china gnome sitting on a china toadstool. He had a bright blue jacket, a pointed red hat, and a long white beard.

'Oh, how sweet!' she said. 'I believe it's an ornament. And there's a letter here too, it says "love from Uncle Michael," I must go and show Mummy.' And off she ran.

'An Ornament,' said Teddy Robinson to himself several times over. 'An Ornament. It sounds rather an important thing to be. More important than Bear or Cat or Dog,' and he began wondering what it was that made an ornament an Ornament, and not just something ordinary.

Deborah came running back.

'Yes,' she said, 'it *is* an ornament. Aren't I lucky? I've had lots of toys, but I've never had an ornament of my own before. I shall keep it here always,' and she put it on the end of the mantelpiece, next to Daddy's pipe-rack.

'But that's where I sit,' said Teddy Robinson.

'Only sometimes,' said Deborah. 'You can sit anywhere because you're a teddy bear. Ornaments have to go on the mantelpiece because they're fragile.'

'Well, that settles it,' said Teddy Robinson. 'I'll be Fragile too. If he sits in my place, then I'll sit in his box. Do you mind lifting me in, very carefully?'

So Deborah lifted him into the box, and Teddy Robinson sat among the straw shavings and felt very precious indeed.

He began singing a little song about it:

> *'Fragile is my middle name,*
> *handle me with care,*
> *Teddy Fragile Robinson,*
> *the ornamental bear.'*

But just then Mummy called to Deborah to bring the box out into the kitchen, because she didn't want the straw shavings all over the carpet. So Teddy Robinson was lifted out again, and that was the last he saw of the box.

He sat on the table and looked up at the china gnome. It wasn't a very friendly looking ornament, but he thought he had better be polite, so he said, 'I hope you're comfortable up there? You get a nice view of everything, being so high up, don't you? I often sit there myself.'

The china gnome didn't even turn his head, but said in a cracked and crusty voice, 'I'm surprised they let you sit up here. The mantelpiece is the place for ornaments, not for toys. I am a very precious and fragile ornament.'

'Well, I'm not exactly a toy,' said Teddy Robinson. 'I am a very precious and fragile teddy bear. I don't wind up or run about on wheels, so you wouldn't exactly call me a toy.'

'Oh, yes, I would,' said the china gnome. 'A soft toy, that's what you are, and you ought to be kept in the toy cupboard. That's the place for soft toys.'

'*Nothing*,' said Teddy Robinson loudly.

'What do you mean?'

'What I say. Deborah's always told me that if I can't

think of a polite answer it's better to say nothing. So that's what I said.'

After that he was quiet for a long while because he was thinking all over again about what it was that made an ornament an Ornament, and not just something ordinary.

'Why are you staring at me like that?' said the china gnome.

'I was wondering what it is you've got that I haven't,' said Teddy Robinson.

'You haven't got a beard, or a pointed hat.'

'No, you're right. I wonder I didn't think of it.'

When Deborah came back again Teddy Robinson said, 'Would you be so kind as to make me a pointed hat?'

'Yes, if you like,' said Deborah, and she made him one out of newspaper.

'And now would you get some cotton wool and some string?'

'What ever for?' said Deborah.

'To make me a beard,' said Teddy Robinson.

So Deborah fetched them, and she did just as Teddy Robinson told her, and put a big lump of cotton wool over the lower part of his face, and tied it round his head with a piece of string.

'Now put me on the mantelpiece,' he said, 'and tell me how many ornaments you see there.'

Deborah stood back and looked at the mantelpiece.

'I see the clock,' she said, 'and Daddy's pipe-rack, and one china ornament, and my dear old teddy bear, with cotton wool all over his face and a paper hat on.'

'Oh,' said Teddy Robinson, 'you're quite sure I don't look like an ornament?'

'Quite sure,' said Deborah, laughing. 'You look rather funny, really.'

'All right,' said Teddy Robinson. 'Take them off again. There's no point in making a fool of myself for nothing.'

Deborah had just taken them off again when there was a ring at the doorbell, and a moment later in came Andrew, Deborah's friend. He admired the china gnome very much, and Deborah told him all about how it had come when she and Teddy Robinson were in the garden.

'And that reminds me,' she said, 'my radishes are nearly ready to be picked. Come and see.'

'I'll just fetch Spotty in,' said Andrew, 'I left him in the hall.'

Spotty was Andrew's toy dog who usually came with him when he came to play with Deborah. Teddy Robinson didn't care for him much because he always wanted to argue, so he quickly put on his Thinking Face and pretended to be making up poetry.

Andrew put them side by side in the arm-chair.

'They can talk to each other while we're busy,' he said.

When the others had gone the spotted dog stared hard at the gnome with his black boot-button eyes, and said rudely, 'That's new. What is it?'

'It's an ornament,' whispered Teddy Robinson.

'Ah, yes, of course. Very useful things, ornaments,' said the spotted dog, who always knew everything.

'What for?' asked Teddy Robinson.

'For being ornamental, of course,' said Spotty.

'Oh,' said Teddy Robinson. 'Yes, of course. What does ornamental mean, exactly?'

'It's what ornaments are,' said Spotty. 'Surely you knew that?'

'Yes,' said Teddy Robinson. 'Of course. I don't know why I asked.'

'Nor do I,' said Spotty. He then stared hard at the china gnome again and barked rudely, 'Hey, Mister Ornament! How do you like living with a teddy bear who doesn't know what ornamental means?'

The china gnome said, in a sharp, cracked voice, 'I

don't like it at all. Neither do I like being shouted at by a rude dog who ought to be outside in a kennel.'

The spotted dog looked very surprised.

'This place seems more like a zoo than a house,' said the china gnome. 'You ought to be outside in the garden.'

'Oh, no,' said Teddy Robinson, 'Spotty isn't a real dog, he's a real *toy* dog; same as I'm not a real bear, but a real *teddy* bear.'

'Then he ought to go in the toy cupboard too,' said the gnome.

There was a rustling noise at the open window, and the Next Door Kitten jumped up on the sill.

'Hallo,' she purred, when she saw Teddy Robinson in the chair. 'Are you coming out?'

'Not just now,' said Teddy Robinson, 'but won't you come in?'

'Thank you,' said the Next Door Kitten, and she jumped through the window and landed on the arm of the chair.

'Who's the old gentleman on the mantelpiece?' she whispered through her whiskers.

'*That,*' said the spotted dog in a loud, rude voice, 'is the ugliest, nastiest –'

But Teddy Robinson said quickly, 'Sssh! He's an ornament. He's come to live here.'

The Next Door Kitten jumped lightly on to the mantelpiece and picked her way carefully along to the china gnome.

'Miaou do you do?' she said politely. 'What purrrfectly lovely weather we're having.'

'Get down! Get down at once!' snapped the china gnome. 'How dare you get up here?'

The Next Door Kitten stepped back, surprised.

'But I often come up here,' she said. 'I come to talk to Teddy Robinson when he's sitting up here.'

'Well, he's not going to sit up here any longer,' said the

gnome. 'I don't like my sitting-room cluttered up with a lot of soft toys. I'm going to arrange for him to live in the toy cupboard. It isn't as if he were an ornament. As for you, get down at once and go back in the garden where you belong. I won't have wild animals in my room.'

'But it's not your room,' said the Next Door Kitten, 'it's Teddy Robinson's, and he invited me in.'

'Yes, I did!' shouted Teddy Robinson from the arm-chair, 'but I never invited you. You just came in a parcel without being asked. I've tried to be polite to you and make you feel at home. I've let you sit in my place on the mantel-piece, but all you've done is be rude to me and my friends, so now I'm not going to try to make you feel at home any more. A gnome in the home is a terrible bore, and I don't want a gnome in my home any more. I shall ask Deborah to have you taken away.'

He stopped for breath; then he said, 'If I wasn't so angry I'd make a song about it. I nearly did by mistake.'

Just then they heard footsteps outside. The Next Door Kitten turned quickly, brushing against the china gnome by mistake, and jumped down off the mantelpiece. At the same minute the china gnome fell with a thud on the carpet.

No one spoke. The Next Door Kitten jumped out of the window, and sat washing her paws quietly on the ledge outside, as if nothing had happened. Then Teddy Robinson peered over the edge of the chair to see what had happened to the china gnome. He was still all in one piece, but there was a long crack down one side of his blue china jacket.

'Poor thing,' said Teddy Robinson kindly, 'I'm afraid you're cracked.'

'Mind your own business,' said the china gnome, and his voice sounded crustier and more cracked than ever. 'I don't talk to soft toys.'

'Well, I may be soft,' said Teddy Robinson, 'but I'm glad I'm not cracked.'

Then the door opened and in came Deborah and Andrew.

'Oh!' said Deborah, 'my ornament has fallen down!'

'And it's cracked down one side,' said Andrew.

'Never mind,' said Mummy, coming in after them, 'it won't show when he's in the garden where he belongs.'

'In the garden?' said Deborah, surprised.

'Yes,' said Mummy, 'he's a garden ornament. Didn't you read Uncle Michael's letter?'

'Oh, no, I forgot!' said Deborah. 'It was such grown-up writing. But I thought he'd sit on the mantelpiece.'

'Oh, no,' said Mummy, 'I don't think he'd look right in here at all, but he'll be lovely in your garden.'

'Oh, yes! He can look after the plants!' said Deborah.

'And frighten the birds away,' said Teddy Robinson.

'Like a scarecrow,' said the spotted dog.

So the china gnome was taken out and put in Deborah's garden, all among the radishes and marigolds, where he really looked quite pretty. Then Deborah found Uncle Michael's letter and read it aloud to Teddy Robinson. It said:

Dear Deborah,

I hope you will like this little gnome for your garden. I think his name must be Grumpy because he looks rather cross, so he may be useful for frightening the slugs and earwigs away. I didn't buy you an indoor ornament because of course you have always got Teddy Robinson.

Love from,
Uncle Michael

'I think that is a very sensible letter,' said Teddy Robinson. 'I always did like Uncle Michael. Can I sit on the mantelpiece again now?'

'Of course,' said Deborah, and she lifted him up.

'There's just one thing more I want to know,' said Teddy

Robinson. 'What exactly *is* an ornament?'

'Why, you funny old boy,' said Deborah. 'Surely you knew that? It's something you put on a shelf because it looks pretty.'

'Well, fancy that!' said Teddy Robinson. 'Then I've been an Ornament all along and I never knew.'

from ANOTHER TEDDY ROBINSON

GRIZZLY BEAR

by Mary Austin

If you ever, ever, ever meet a grizzly bear,
You must never, never, never ask him *where*
He is going,
Or *what* he is doing;
For if you ever, ever dare
To stop a grizzly bear,
You will never meet *another* grizzly bear.

from THE CHILDREN SING IN THE FAR WEST

THE THREE BEARS

Once upon a time there were Three Bears. Father Bear was a great big gruff bear. Mother Bear was a plump, medium-sized fluffy bear. Then there was Baby Bear, who was a little teeny weeny small furry bear. These Three Bears lived in a little cottage in the middle of a wood.

Now in the village at the edge of the wood there lived a little girl whose name was Goldilocks, for her hair was the colour of spun gold. She had never met the Three Bears, since they were shy creatures and kept very much to themselves. The bears had regular dealings with the village grocer, since they were VERY fond of porridge and ate it at every meal, but apart from the grocer no one in the village had met them.

One day, however, Goldilocks and the Three Bears did meet, and it would be hard to say who was the most surprised.

On the morning of which I am speaking, Goldilocks got up very early indeed and went into the woods to look for mushrooms.

The Three Bears were just about to eat their breakfast. Father Bear and Baby Bear licked their lips hungrily as Mother Bear ladled porridge into three bowls. There was a great big enormous bowl for Father Bear, a medium-sized bowl for Mother Bear herself, and a little teeny weeny bowl for Baby Bear. The porridge was boiling hot, so the Three Bears decided to go for a brisk healthy walk while their porridge was cooling.

Meanwhile, Goldilocks had got lost in the woods. She found herself walking up the path leading to the Three Bears' cottage, so she decided to go and ask the way back to the village. She knocked at the cottage door, but since no

one answered she pushed the door open and went inside, for by now she was feeling very tired.

The first thing Goldilocks saw as she entered the cottage was the table set with three bowls of steaming hot porridge. Goldilocks forgot that the porridge must be someone else's breakfast. All she could think of was how ravenously hungry she felt herself.

Goldilocks took a spoonful of porridge from the biggest bowl. But Father Bear had sprinkled salt on his porridge. Although that was how Father Bear liked to eat it, Goldilocks put the spoon down with a wry face. Next she tasted a spoonful of porridge from the medium-sized bowl. But there was no sugar on it, since Mother Bear was worrying about getting stout and had decided not to eat sweet things. So Goldilocks put that spoon down in disgust, too. Then Goldilocks cautiously tried a spoonful of porridge from the little teeny weeny bowl. Baby Bear had poured syrup and cream all over his porridge, and it was so delicious that Goldilocks ate up every mouthful of Baby Bear's breakfast.

When she had finished, Goldilocks decided to wait for someone to come home who would tell her how to get back to her home in the village. First she sat on Father Bear's great big enormous chair, but it was too hard and un-comfortable. Next she sat in Mother Bear's medium-sized chair, but there were too many cushions and the feathers tickled her nose and made her sneeze, so she climbed off and sat in Baby Bear's teeny weeny chair. It was just right, but Goldilocks was too heavy for it and one of the legs broke. Goldilocks was thrown – BUMP! – onto the floor.

Goldilocks was sore and cross when she got to her feet, so she went upstairs to find somewhere to rest. First she tried to scramble up on to Father Bear's great big enormous bed, but it was too high and she couldn't reach. Next she climbed into Mother Bear's medium-sized bed, but it was much too soft for her, and Goldilocks disappeared in a mound of pillows and matresses and eiderdowns. She kicked and struggled to get free and landed – BUMP! – on the floor again. After that she just rolled straight into Baby Bear's little teeny weeny bed. It was just right and Goldilocks fell asleep immediately.

After their walk the Three Bears came back to their cottage, eagerly looking forward to their breakfast. When they saw their bowls on the table they all three threw up their paws and exclaimed with astonishment.

'Somebody's been eating my porridge' said Father Bear in his deep gruff voice.

'Somebody's been eating *my* porridge' said Mother Bear in surprise.

'Somebody's been eating *my* porridge *and* eaten it *all* up!' squealed Baby Bear in his high squeaky little voice.

The Three Bears sat down in their chairs to think over the intrusion they had discovered.

'Somebody's been sitting in my chair' growled Father Bear.

'Somebody's been sitting in *my* chair' said Mother Bear.

'Somebody's been sitting in *my* chair *and* broken it *all* up!' cried Baby Bear.

Then the Three Bears went upstairs to see what was going on up there.

'Somebody's been sleeping in my bed' said Father Bear.

'Somebody's been sleeping in *my* bed' echoed Mother Bear.

'Somebody's been sleeping in *my* bed *and* that somebody is *still* there!' piped Baby Bear.

The Three Bears made such a clatter that Goldilocks woke up. She was so frightened when she saw the Three Bears staring at her that she leapt out of Baby Bear's bed and ran down the stairs and straight out of the house, and she didn't stop running until she was out of the wood. She could see her village in the distance and she raced all the way home to tell her family about her adventure.

Mother Bear made some more porridge when the Three Bears had got over their shock, and for lunch they ate the mushrooms that Goldilocks had left behind in her hurry to get away.

TRADITIONAL

THREE OLD FABLES

This first story is an old Greek fable recounted by Æsop

A bear was once boasting what a kind, good-natured fellow he was. 'I know no one,' he said proudly, 'who is nicer than I am. How lucky the other animals are to have me for a friend! They all know the tradition that a bear would never touch or harm a dead body, and they love me for it.'

A fox heard the bear boasting and laughed. 'On the contrary, Bear,' said the fox, 'we wish that when you feel hungry you *would* only touch the dead, and leave us living animals alone!'

The second story comes from Bulgaria

One day a farmer went into the forest to cut wood. Suddenly he heard a whimper and, hurrying through the trees, he came upon a she-bear whose paw was caught fast in a trap.

The she-bear called out to the farmer 'Please help me to escape from this cruel trap. I have been here all night and was despairing of being rescued. I promise I shan't harm you, but for pity's sake help me to get free.'

The farmer did his best to help the bear and prised the trap open with his axe. The bear snatched her paw out of the trap, and danced in circles round the farmer in her happiness and delight at being free. Then, rising on her hind legs, she embraced the farmer and covered his face with kisses.

'Get away!' cried the farmer, struggling to get free himself. 'You smell horribly of bear and I don't like your kissing me'.

The bear backed away immediately and tears came into her eyes. 'You shouldn't have said such an unkind thing' she cried. 'Hit me quickly with your axe, or I shall become angry and eat you.'

The frightened farmer hit out at the bear with his axe. The bear immediately ran off into the heart of the forest, but the farmer could see blood on her shoulder.

One year later the farmer was again in the forest, cutting wood. Suddenly he felt a soft tap on his arm and, turning, he found himself face-to-face with the she-bear.

'Look at my shoulder,' she said, 'where you wounded me with your axe.'

The farmer looked at the bear's shoulder, but the wound had quite healed and the fur had grown again, so that he could not tell at all where she had been hurt.

'But the wound in my heart caused by your unkind words

has not healed' said the bear. 'The wound from an axe will disappear and leave no trace, but the wound left by a harsh word remains for ever.'

The third story is an old Norse tale

A bear and a fox once decided to go into partnership. 'With my brains and your strength' said the fox, 'we are sure to make our fortunes.'

So the bear and the fox became farmers. 'We must be sure,' said the fox, 'to divide our crops equally between us. To be certain we divide things fairly, why don't you take everything that grows above the earth, and I will content myself with the roots that grow beneath the earth.' This seemed a good idea to the bear, and he agreed.

That first year the bear and the fox planted turnips. The bear was happy when he saw all the green leaves. He cut them all and tied them in bundles. Then he took them into the market and tried to sell them. Much to the bear's surprise, however, no one would buy his leaves. Then he noticed a crowd róund another stall. When the bear went over to look, he found the fox doing a brisk trade selling the turnips he had dug up from the ground.

'Fox, you have cheated me,' complained the bear angrily. 'You have sold your turnips easily enough and are now rich, but no one wanted my leaves and I have made no money at all.'

'But we agreed to divide everything fairly,' cried the fox. 'When we gather the next crop, it will be your turn to have whatever grows below the earth, and my turn to take whatever grows on top.' The bear felt better when the fox had explained this, and agreed to go into partnership with the fox again. 'I am only thinking of you,' said the crafty fox, 'and I would like to suggest that this time we plant corn, since that should make us both rich.' The bear thought this would be a good crop, and looked forward to making his fortune.

When the corn ripened, however, the crafty fox cut the sheaves and took them to market where he made a lot of money. The bear dug hard to get the roots out of the earth, but when he tried to sell them in the market the people just laughed at him. 'What good are roots for eating, you silly Bear!' they shouted.

Do you think that the bear went into partnership with the fox a third time?

TRADITIONAL

SNOW-WHITE
AND ROSE-RED

There once was a widow who lived with her two daughters in a little cottage near a forest. In her garden there grew two rose bushes, one bearing red roses and the other white roses. The widow called her daughters Snow-White and Rose-Red after these two rose bushes.

Every morning in the summer Rose-Red would gather a big bunch of roses to decorate the cottage, and their fragrance filled every room. Rose-Red was gay and was always laughing and joking. She was afraid of nothing and loved to run in the fields in the sunshine, and look for wild flowers and butterflies.

Snow-White was a shy, gentle girl. She preferred to stay at home and help her mother. In the summer she would sweep out the cottage and watch the seeds she had planted in the garden grow into strong plants bearing red, yellow and blue flowers. In winter Rose-Red would help Snow-White to polish the big copper kettle and the saucepans until they shone, and to do the cooking for their mother.

Although the two daughters were so different, they loved each other dearly and spent many happy hours together, wandering in the forest. The forest animals knew them: the birds flew down to eat bread from their hands, and the rabbits and deer gathered round to greet them.

When winter came, the snow lay thick around the little cottage. One evening Snow-White and Rose-Red were sitting with their toes stretched out toward the brightly burning fire. Their mother got out her knitting and Snow-White began to read a story in the flickering fire-light. Suddenly there was a loud knock at the cottage door.

'Whoever can that be?' cried the girls in surprise. 'It's very late for visitors on such a cold night.'

'Go and open the door, Rose-Red' said her mother. 'It must be a traveller who has lost his way in the dark.'

So Rose-Red went to the door and drew back the bolts. But when she opened the door she jumped back in surprise, for there on the doorstep was a huge furry bear. His shaggy coat was covered with snowflakes and the wind whistled round him and rushed into the cottage, bringing with it a shower of snow.

Snow-White and Rose-Red were so frightened to see the bear that they hid themselves under the bed in the corner. But the bear ambled into the room and said 'Please do not be afraid. I will not do you any harm. I only wish to lie for a little while by your fire, for it is bitterly cold out in the forest and I am frozen through.'

'You poor creature,' cried the girls' mother. 'You are welcome to stay here for the night in the warm.'

Seeing that there was no need to fear the bear, the children came out from under the bed. Taking the broom from the corner, they began to brush the snow from the bear's furry coat.

After that, the bear soon became a well-loved member of the family. The cottage door was always left unbolted until he had come home in the evening, and then the girls would play with him by the fireside. They brushed his thick coat until it was sleek and shining, and he gave them rides round the kitchen on his broad back. When they were tired the bear would tell Snow-White and Rose-Red stories about the animals and the strange fairy people who lived in the heart of the forest.

When spring came, however, and the snow had all disappeared, the bear told them that he must return to the forest for good. Snow-White and Rose-Red and their mother were very sad to lose their friend. They waved good-bye to him from the cottage gate, and watched as he ambled off into the trees. They did not know whether they would be able to see the bear again.

One day soon afterward Snow-White and Rose-Red went together into the forest to look for wild strawberries. Suddenly they heard a hideous shriek. They hurried into a clearing and found a little old goblin leaping up and down in fury. They soon saw that he had been cutting wood and had got the end of his long white beard caught and tangled in one of the tree's roots.

The girls ran forward and tried to help the goblin to free himself. But his beard was so tightly knotted and twisted that the only way was to cut off the end. So Rose-Red took out her scissors and snipped off the tangled bits of beard.

As soon as the goblin was free, he turned all his fury on to the two girls. 'You fools, you silly meddling ninnies' he shrieked. 'You've ruined my looks by hacking at my beautiful beard!' And, grabbing a bag of gold pieces that had been hidden under the tree, he ran off into the forest. Snow-White and Rose-Red looked at one another in amazement. Then they burst out laughing at the little man's rudeness, and continued on their way.

Some weeks later, Snow-White and Rose-Red went down to the lake to catch a fish for supper. As they neared the lake, they saw that the little old goblin was there before them, and that he was leaping up and down and waving his arms wildly. He was fishing too, and had caught an enormous fish on the end of his line. But his long white beard had got tangled in his fishing line, and the strong fish was dragging him into the water as it struggled to get free. The girls ran up and the old man shouted, 'Don't just stand there! Can't you do anything to help me?'

Snow-White and Rose-Red did their best to free the goblin, but his long beard was so twisted round and caught up in the fishing line that they could not get it free. The old man was being dragged deeper and deeper into the water. At last Rose-Red decided that there was nothing else for it. She got out her scissors and snipped off the end of the old man's beard, just before he disappeared below the water.

When he got out of the water the old man was purple with fury. 'You stupid, wicked girls!' he yelled. 'You've cut off all my beautiful beard! Everyone will laugh at me now, thanks to you! I hope I never see you again!' He picked up a sack of diamonds which he had left on the bank, and ran off into the bushes, grumbling under his breath.

Snow-White and Rose-Red were hurt by the goblin's ingratitude, but he had looked so funny in the water that they soon began to laugh, and forgot all about him.

A few days later, however, Snow-White and Rose-Red went out into the fields to look for blackberries in the hedgerows. Once more they heard the goblin's piercing shriek, and whirling round they saw him in the middle of the field. An eagle had also spotted him and, thinking that he would be a tasty morsel, had swooped down. Grasping the goblin with his talons, the eagle was bearing him off into the sky. Snow-White and Rose-Red ran over in answer to the goblin's terrified cries. They were just in time to catch the goblin's feet and to pull him from the eagle's grip. The old man fell with a bump onto the ground. He sat up angrily and looked at his mud-stained coat.

'You clumsy fools!' he exclaimed. 'You've torn my beautiful smart coat! Why can't you ever keep out of my way and mind your own business?' So saying, he gathered up a bagful of pearls which had dropped out of his pocket, and ran off, shaking his fist.

Rose-Red and Snow-White were not allowed to forget the goblin, however. When they had picked as many black-berries as they could carry, they set off for home. Suddenly they came upon the little old goblin. He was crouching under a thorn bush and, thinking that he was hidden from sight, he had spread all his gold and jewels on the ground. He had silver and gold pieces, diamonds, rubies, emeralds and pearls, and his eyes gleamed greedily as he ran his hands over his treasure. He was singing a little gloating song, but he left off sharply as he saw that Snow-White and Rose-Red were standing staring at him, unable to take their eyes off all his glittering hoard. The goblin leaped up in rage and lunged towards the two girls.

'Go away, go away!' he screamed. 'I'll teach you to come interfering and spying and prying!'

Snow-White and Rose-Red were very frightened and started to run away as fast as they could, the goblin following them on his little short legs. Suddenly they heard a fierce growl and a huge bear leapt from the bushes and grasped the goblin.

Then it was the goblin's turn to be frightened. He cringed on the ground at the bear's feet and cried 'Nice, kind bear! Please don't harm me, dear, sweet bear! If you're hungry, don't bother with me, since I am old and thin and tough. Why don't you eat those two tender young girls? There would be far more meat on them! Please don't hurt me!'

But the bear paid no attention to the goblin's words. With one swing of his paw he put an end to the old man and, as he did so, his shaggy fur fell away. In the bear's place there stepped forward a handsome young man in clothes of shining gold.

'Do not be afraid, Snow-White and Rose-Red' said he. 'I am the bear you befriended all during the long cold winter, and I shall try to repay all your kindness to me now that I am free. This wicked old goblin had cast a spell upon me and turned me into a bear, so that he could enjoy all my riches. Only his death could set me free, and now he is powerless to harm me any more.'

When the prince returned to his own kingdom there was great rejoicing. He was true to his word and made sure that Snow-White, Rose-Red and their mother should never want for anything. And after a few years, the prince took Snow-White as his wife, and the prince's brother married Rose-Red. They all lived in the prince's castle, while the girls' mother had a little cottage in the castle grounds. In her garden grew two rose-bushes, one bearing red roses and the other white roses, and they filled the cottage and its garden with fragrance.

TRADITIONAL

THE DOG AND THE BEAR

by John Yeoman

One day a peasant said to his dog: 'You are getting too old and lazy to guard my chickens and my house. I will buy myself a new dog, a young dog, and you can go off to the forest to live, for I am not going to feed you any longer.'

And so the poor old dog, who had been very faithful to his master, went sadly into the forest. He had always had his food and drink put down for him in little enamel bowls and after hours of searching could not find anything to eat in the forest.

At last a kindly bear ambled past.

'Please, bear, I have been turned out into the dark forest to find my own food, and there seems to be nothing to eat here at all.'

The bear was very sorry for the poor dog and offered him a bees' nest. 'Have some honey,' he said. 'It's good for the voice.'

The dog gratefully thrust his tongue into the nest, but all the honey got up his nose and made him sneeze. 'I don't think dogs eat honey,' he said miserably. 'Haven't you any meat?'

The bear hadn't any meat, but he said that if the dog would like to be his partner, between them they could have all the meat they wanted. The dog would have to do the hunting and the bear, who was as strong as any animal in the forest, would do the killing. But both agreed that this would be hard work.

Suddenly the bear sat up with a look of triumph on his face. 'I have a wonderful idea,' he said. 'We will got to your old master's house and I will creep up to the cot that stands on the porch and snatch the baby from it. Then you will chase me and I will pretend to be frightened and run away. When you return the baby to its parents, they will be so grateful that you will get your old job back again.'

'It sounds better than working for a living,' said the dog. 'But what do you get out of it?'

The bear looked wise and said: 'I'll scratch your back; you scratch mine.' So the dog scratched the bear's broad back, although he still did not understand how the plan would help the bear.

Next day the huge bear tiptoed up to the baby's cot, lifted the baby gently in his great paws and stuck his head in at the window of the house, making a fearful roar as he did so. The mother screamed and rushed out, waving a broom. But the bear lumbered off, faster than she could run. The new dog was afraid of such a big, fierce animal, and he would not come out of his kennel. But our dog, waiting for the right moment, ran from behind the house, barking for all he was worth, and caught up with the bear. The bear stopped in his tracks, laid the baby carefully on the ground, rose awkwardly on his back legs, raised his arms above his head, and said, 'Heaven save us; a dog!' Then he shuffled away while the dog took the baby back to its mother. When her husband came in from the fields he said: 'I was wrong. There is life in the old dog yet. He shall have his job back again.'

Once more the dog was given all the food and drink he wanted in enamel bowls. One day, when he was lazing in the sun with one eye on the chickens, the bear appeared.

'Now,' said the bear, 'it is your turn to help me. Your master and his wife are giving a party to a few of their friends in there, and you must invite me in, too.'

'I can't,' said the dog, 'for someone would be sure to see you.'

'I will sit at the back,' said the bear.

So they went into the house very quietly, without anyone noticing, and the bear sat on a chair behind everyone else, in a dark corner. Everybody was so busy talking and eating and drinking that they did not bother to look round at him, although from time to time they passed him cups of tea and fancy iced pastries over their shoulders.

But at last the guests began to sing songs, clapping their hands to the music, and this was too much for the bear. He loved singing, and could not help joining in. The louder the guests sang, the louder he sang (but not the same song, because he only knew bear songs). In the end he was so excited that he was lifting his knees and pounding his feet on the floor. 'Fmoo, fmoo!' he roared at the top of his voice, which, as you know, is bear singing. Suddenly, too suddenly for the bear, the guests finished their song, only to be amazed by the row coming from the dark corner.

'It's a bear!' cried someone. 'The same bear!' cried someone else. 'That dog brought him in!' they all screamed. 'They must have been friends all the time!' And they all got brooms and shovels and mops and sticks and chased the bear and the dog back into the forest.

In the forest they were kept very busy in their search for food, although they still had time enough to scratch each other's back occasionally.

from A DRINK OF WATER AND OTHER STORIES

THE SHE-BEAR

by Ruth Manning-Sanders

There was once a pretty little princess called Luciella. And early one morning the king, her father, sent for her and said, 'Luciella, dress yourself in your best robes and put jewels in your hair, for today King Pippo is coming to ask your hand in marriage.'

'But Papa, Papa,' cried Luciella, 'King Pippo is old and ugly, and I've heard that he has a very bad temper. I don't want to marry him!'

'You will do as you're told,' said her father. 'King Pippo is the richest monarch in all the world. I have but a little kingdom, King Pippo has a big one. If you don't marry him, King Pippo will make war on me and take my little kingdom from me. So go along, and make yourself ready to receive him.'

Princess Luciella ran out into the garden. She sat down under a rose bush and cried. 'I won't marry the ugly old thing,' she sobbed. 'I won't, I *won't!*'

And out from behind the rose bush stepped a tiny old man with a long white beard.

Said he, 'Little princess, pretty little princess, why are you crying?'

'Oh! Oh! Oh! My father says I must marry ugly old King Pippo, and I don't want to!'

'Well, if you don't want to marry him, you needn't,' said the tiny man. And he gave Luciella a little stick. 'Put this stick in your mouth,' said he, 'and it will turn you into a bear. I don't think King Pippo will want to marry a she-bear!'

'No, I'm sure he won't!' laughed Luciella. And she took the little stick, gave the tiny man a kiss, and ran back into the palace.

That very morning ugly old King Pippo arrived. He scowled round at everybody and said, 'Where's my bride?'

'Her maidens are just now robing her,' said Luciella's father. 'She will be down immediately.'

'Then tell her to hurry herself,' said King Pippo rudely.

So a page was sent scurrying upstairs to the princess's room, where her maidens, having dressed her in a white robe trimmed with pearls, had just finished combing out her long golden hair, and were now setting a little crown of diamonds on her head.

Princess Luciella peeped at herself in the mirror and laughed. 'Do I look pretty?' she asked.

'You look most beautiful,' said the maidens.

The princess laughed again.

'And will King Pippo be pleased with me?'

'Indeed he cannot fail to be pleased,' said the maidens. But they thought, 'Oh what a shame to give our darling princess to that ugly old wretch! And she laughs! How can she laugh?'

'Now bring me downstairs,' said Luciella.

The maidens brought the laughing Luciella downstairs. The doors of the great hall were flung open. Musicians played softly. 'Her Royal Highness the princess Luciella!' cried the king's herald.

But what should come ambling in but a huge, shaggy

she-bear: for princess Luciella had put the little stick in her mouth.

'Ah-ah-ah!' The ladies screamed and ran. The lords and the pages jumped out of the windows. The princess's father dived under the table. *Gr-gr-gr!* The bear ran about the hall, growling and snarling. King Pippo drew his sword. The bear stood on her hind legs and landed him a box on the ear that sent him sprawling. Then she gave a roar that set all the gold and silver dishes tinkling, and ran out of the palace.

'You will live to repent of this insult!' shouted King Pippo to the princess's father. And he went home in a rage.

Meanwhile Luciella Bear was running, running. She ran till she came to a great forest. And in that forest she lived happily, feeding on honey and wild berries. The little stick in her mouth didn't worry her; it was so small that she could hold it easily in her cheek.

But one day she heard the sounds of hurrying footsteps. Who was coming? An enemy? Perhaps King Pippo himself! Luciella Bear hid behind a tree and watched. No, it wasn't King Pippo. It was a young prince who had lost his way and was wandering here and there in the hope of finding a path to lead him home.

But he didn't find a path to lead him home. All he found was a great shaggy she-bear, who leaped from behind the tree and came bounding towards him.

The prince was frightened: the bear was so very huge, and he was unarmed, except for a little dagger at his belt. But he drew that little dagger, and stood his ground manfully.

'If I am to die, I will at least die fighting!' he thought.

But what was this? The bear lay down at his feet, rolled over on her side, and wagged her stump of a tail. For the prince was very handsome, and Luciella Bear hadn't seen a human being for a long, long time; and glad indeed she was to see one now, and that one so much to her liking.

So, as she went on wagging her tail, and looking up at the prince with admiring eyes, he lost all fear of her. He stooped and patted her head. He took some cake from his wallet and held it out to her. And what did Luciella Bear do then? She sat up and begged.

The prince laughed. 'Well, my bear, I see that someone has taught you good manners. I think you haven't always lived in the wild. I think you must have been somebody's pet. So, what do you say – will you be my pet now, and come home with me?'

And Luciella Bear nodded her head, and said '*Hou-oom, gr-oum,*' which was the nearest she could get to 'yes'.

'Only, my bear,' said the prince, 'the trouble is I'm lost. I don't know the way out of this forest.'

Oh, but Luciella Bear knew the way, and this she tried to tell him with so many gruntings and noddings of her head and waving of her paws, that when she began walking away the prince followed her; and she soon brought him the quickest way out of the forest and back into his own kingdom.

And there they are now, walking side by side, the prince with his hand on Luciella Bear's head. And so he brought her to his palace.

The young prince was delighted with his new pet. He had a pretty little house built for her in the palace garden, by a fountain just under the window of his bedroom, so that he could look out and call to her first thing in the morning and last thing at night. He fed her with his own hands, and ordered everyone to treat her with the greatest respect. And she went in and out of her little house, just as she pleased, and drank from the fountain, and wandered about the garden at her will, and was so very gentle and charming in her ways that all the prince's servants came to love her.

Now by and by it came summertime and very hot, and Luciella Bear panted with the heat inside her thick coat. So early one morning, before anyone was up, she took the stick out of her mouth and turned into a girl again. And the girl went to the fountain and bathed her hands and face. Then she sat down on the edge of the fountain, took a comb from her pocket and began combing out her long golden hair. And the rising sun shone on that golden hair and made a glory of it. And whilst she combed her hair, princess Luciella was singing to herself, very very softly, for she was thinking that no one could see or hear her.

But someone did see and hear her, and that was the prince. For he too had felt stifled by the heat, and he had risen from his bed. There he was now, standing at his open window, looking down into the garden.

And what does the prince see down there, down there in the garden? He sees a maiden more beautiful than he had ever imagined a maiden could be. 'Oh! Oh!' He turns from

the window, runs downstairs, and out at the great palace door.

But in his hurry he didn't think to open that door quietly, and the clatter he made startled Luciella, and quicker than quick she snatched up the stick and put it back into her mouth; so that all the prince saw when he ran to the fountain was his great shaggy bear ambling to meet him with love in her eyes.

'No, no, dear bear, it's not you I want!' cried the prince. 'The maiden, the maiden, where has she gone? Oh, my bear, you must have seen her! As you love me, lead me to her, my bear, and I'll give you a golden collar with diamond studs!'

But Luciella Bear turned her back on him and went into her little house, and the prince ran about the garden, searching, searching. Of course he didn't find the maiden, though he had all his servants searching for her till nightfall. So what happened? He took to his bed and fell into a fever, and not a doctor in the kingdom could cure him.

In his fevered dreams it seemed to the prince that he was out in the garden again, running after a maiden, and that he was just about to catch her when she laughed and turned into a bear. And he woke, flinging out his arms and crying, 'Oh, my bear, my bear, my cruel, cruel bear!'

Now it so happened that the queen, his mother, was standing by his bed when he called out. And she said to herself, 'Then it is the bear who has caused my son's sickness! The creature must be a witch who has cast an evil spell on him!'

Then the queen hurried out of the prince's room, summoned a groom to her and said, 'Take a sword and kill that bear at once!'

But the groom isn't going to kill the bear, not he! He's much too fond of her. So what does he do? He coaxes her away into the forest with sweet cakes, ties her to a tree and lays a pile of food at her feet. 'I will come every day and feed you,' says he, and so leaves her.

The queen was watching by the prince's bed. 'As soon as the bear is dead, his sickness will leave him,' she thought. 'Oh, my son, my dear son, in a few moments now you will be yourself again!'

And she sent a page to bring the groom up to her; and when he came she whispered, 'Have you killed the bear?'

The groom looks her straight in the eyes, and lies bravely. 'Yes, your majesty, I have killed the bear.'

The prince hears, he gives a shout, leaps from his bed, snatches up his sword and runs at the groom. 'You murderer of all my hopes! Now you shall die, and when I have killed you, I will kill myself!'

The queen screams, the groom cries out in panic, 'No, no, my prince, I lied, I lied! I haven't killed your bear – how could I do such a cruel thing? I have only taken her into the forest and left her there, tied to a tree.'

Sick as he was, the prince huddled on some clothes, staggered from the room and down to the stables, scrambled on to his horse, more dead than alive, and galloped off to the forest. There he found his bear, and sobbing with pity and relief, he cut the rope that bound her, and brought her back to the palace.

She was glad enough to follow him.

By the time the prince had got back into the garden, he was raving again, and he cried to her, 'My bear, my bear, take off your skin, take off your skin! If you love me at all, if you wish me to live and not to die, *take off your skin!*'

But Luciella Bear walked away into her little house.

So then the prince flung himself back to bed, turned his face to the wall, and wept. And the queen, his mother, came and sat by the bed. 'My dear son, what causes this heart-breaking grief? Tell me, only tell me, that I may help and comfort you!'

And the prince answered, 'Nothing can comfort me but my bear. If you want me to live, have her brought to my room. I want no one else to look after me, I want no one else to smooth my bed, I want no one else to cook my food, I want no one else to tidy my room, but only my bear.'

'This is madness!' thought the queen. But she had the bear brought to his room. And the bear came over to the bed. She took the prince's hand between her great paws.

And the prince smiled. 'My bear,' said he, 'it is a long time since I tasted food. But if *you* would cook me something, I believe I would eat it. Won't you cook me something, my darling bear?'

'*Hou-oum, gr-oum,*' said Luciella Bear, nodding her head.

'Mother,' said the prince, 'send for a cooking stove and a pan, and a chicken and herbs and seasoning.'

'Oh, my poor son, he is quite, quite crazy!' thinks the queen. But she did what he asked her.

So there was the stove, and the bear lit it. There was the pan, and the bear put it on the stove. There was the chicken, and the bear put it in the pan with the herbs and the seasoning. And when the chicken was cooked, the bear laid it neatly in a dish, and brought it to the prince. And the prince, who for days had not been able to swallow down so much as a spoonful of soup, ate up everything, scraped the dish, and licked his fingers.

'That was the most delicious food I have ever tasted!' said he.

So, when he had finished eating, the bear handed him a glass of wine, and she did it with so much grace that the queen felt ready to kiss her. As for the prince, he jumped out of bed and put on his clothes; and the bear re-made the bed, and tidied up the room; and then she went into the garden, and came back with great armfuls of roses; these she strewed all over the bed. And the queen thought, 'This bear is indeed a treasure! No wonder my son loves her!'

But the prince has remembered his dreams again. He turns pale as death. 'Oh, my lady mother,' he cries, 'if my bear will not kiss me, I believe my spirit will leave my body!'

And the queen, fearing to see her son fall into a mad fit again, said to the bear, 'My dear creature, kiss him, kiss him quickly!'

Luciella Bear goes to the prince; she lays her muzzle against his face. The prince seizes her by both cheeks. What happens? The stick falls out of the bear's mouth – and there is the prince holding in his arms the most beautiful princess that ever the sun shone on.

'Oh, my love, my love, my love, I have found you at last!'

'Yes,' laughed princess Luciella, 'you have found me!' And she told him all her sad little story. And just as the story had come to an end, who should jump out from among the heap of roses on the bed, but the tiny old man with the long white beard.

'Princess, pretty little princess,' says he, 'once I saw you crying, now I see you laughing. You won't want my stick any more, so I'll take it back again.' And take it back he did. 'All stories should have happy endings,' says he, as he hops through the window. 'And what happier ending can there be than that a lovely princess should marry a handsome prince?'

The lovely princess did marry the handsome prince. The king, the princess's father, came to the wedding. Poor man, he had been living in fear all this time, lest King Pippo should send an army and take his little kingdom from him. But the prince said, 'I have a bigger army even than King Pippo, and I am on your side. Let King Pippo come if he dare!'

King Pippo didn't dare. So the prince, the princess and the princess's father lived in peace and happiness all their lives.

from A BOOK OF PRINCES AND PRINCESSES

THE POLAR BEAR

by Magnus Magnusson

Iceland isn't such a cold country as its name suggests, and certainly it isn't nearly cold enough for polar bears. Polar bears come from still farther north, in Greenland, and before there were any zoos they were a very rare sight in the warmer lands. They were highly prized because of their beautiful fur, although in the old days only kings could afford to keep such huge animals.

Once long ago in Iceland, there lived a man whose name

was Audun. He wasn't very rich, but he made his living by working on farms and sometimes as a seaman. He was a good worker, and very loyal, and one year the farmer he worked for gave him a present of a holiday, and a voyage on a ship that was travelling round the northern countries.

Audun arranged for his mother to be looked after while he was away, and paid for everything she would need for three years; and he took the rest of his savings with him, because he knew what he wanted to do.

He wanted to buy a polar bear and give it as a present to the King of Denmark. Now, this sounds rather a surprising thing to do. Audun didn't know the King of Denmark, nor was the King of Denmark *his* King. But he thought the King of Denmark, King Svein, was the most just and kind ruler in the world, and he wanted to do something special for him to show his admiration.

The ship went to Greenland where there were plenty of polar bears. There Audun spent all his savings on a wonderful bear, which had a thick coat of beautiful white fur. Audun's ship now set off for Denmark. But on the way it stopped in Norway for some time, and Audun had to wait there.

A polar bear was a rare sight in Norway, and before long King Harald of Norway heard about it. King Harald was a fierce Viking who liked to have his own way in everything. So he sent for Audun and offered to buy it. 'Will you sell the bear for the same price you paid for it?' asked the King.

'I don't want to sell it, sire,' said Audun.

'What if I offer you twice the price you paid for it?' asked the King.

Audun still said he didn't want to sell it.

'Well, do you want to *give* it to me?' asked the King – and he would have given Audun a wonderful gift in exchange.

But Audun said no. So the King asked him what he was going to do with the bear – and Audun said, quite honestly, that he was going to give it to the King of Denmark.

Audun really was very honest and brave to say that, because Norway and Denmark were at war at the time, and the two Kings hated each other.

The King of Norway looked at him and thought he must be mad, telling him a thing like that; but he couldn't help admiring someone who made up his mind and stuck to his decision whatever the dangers. So he didn't imprison Audun, or punish him, but wished him good luck and sent him on his way, unharmed.

But the King did make one condition – he made Audun promise to come back and tell him how the King of Denmark had rewarded him for such a wonderful gift. And this Audun promised to do.

So Audun went to Denmark. But when he arrived he had no money left at all and couldn't buy any food for himself or the bear, which ate a tremendous amount. So he went to see the King of Denmark's steward, Aki, who was a most important man.

But Aki proposed a very unfair bargain. He said he would give Audun money for food – but only if Audun would give him a half-share in the bear, so that Audun's present to the King of Denmark would become a present from both of them.

Poor Audun had no choice; if he didn't agree, the bear and he would simply die of starvation.

A few days later he was granted an audience with the King of Denmark, and went to see him with the bear. The King asked him what he wanted, and Audun explained.

'I am an Icelander, sire,' he said, 'and I have just come from Greenland, after a short stay in Norway. I had been meaning to present you with this bear, which I bought with every penny I had, but now I cannot do this because I own only half of him.' And he told the King about the deal he had made with Aki.

The King was delighted with the present, but he was very

angry with Aki, and dismissed him at once and banished him from the kingdom. Audun, however, was invited to stay at court as an honoured guest. But there remained one other thing that Audun wanted to do – he wanted to travel to Rome, the chief city of the Christian world, to pray there with other Christian pilgrims from all over Europe.

The King of Denmark gave him money to cover his costs, and Audun set off on his pilgrimage. He got to Rome safely, but then he fell ill.

His money was all spent as he lay sick in bed, and he became very thin. The only way he could get back to Denmark was by begging for money to pay for his journey. But when at last Audun got back, he was so poor and ill that he didn't dare go to see the King, he felt so ashamed. Then on Easter Sunday he went to church.

The King was there; and although Audun didn't have the courage to speak up, the King felt there was someone there who wanted to speak to him. He picked out Audun even though he didn't recognize him any longer. But when at last he realised that this pitiful beggar was the man who had once given him the polar bear, he took him home to the palace as an honoured guest.

The following spring, Audun wanted to return to Iceland. The King of Denmark was very surprised – until Audun explained that his mother would be running short of money by now. Audun didn't want to live in the lap of luxury while his mother starved. So the King understood at once, and praised his thoughtfulness, and gave him permission to leave.

One day he took Audun down to the harbour, where ships of all kinds were being made ready to sail away on trading voyages. They stopped beside one particularly fine ship and the King said to Audun: 'What do you think of that ship?'

'It's a very fine ship,' said Audun.

And the King said: 'I'm going to give you that ship and all

its cargo, as a reward for the polar bear you once gave me.'

What a marvellous present! A whole ship and its cargo, in return for a polar bear! But it wasn't the polar bear that the King was rewarding – it was Audun's courage and honesty.

But that was not the end of the story. Because the King then said: 'I've heard that your country has a dangerous coastline, and that you might be shipwrecked. If you are shipwrecked and lose the ship and the cargo, you would have nothing to show that you met the King of Denmark and were given a fine gift. So I'm also going to give you a big purse of silver. But just in case you lose this purse as well, I'm going to give you something else.' And with that he unclasped a solid silver armlet he was wearing and gave it to Audun. And he said: 'Even if you lose everything else, you will always have this royal gift. I urge you never to give it away to anyone – unless it is to some great man to whom you feel you owe a great debt.'

The King said farewell, and Audun sailed away. But Audun always kept his promises, and so he went to visit the King of Norway on his way back to Iceland.

The King of Norway was very curious to know what had happened to Audun in Denmark. 'How did King Svein reward you for the polar bear?' asked the King.

'By accepting it, sire,' said Audun.

'I would have done that too. Didn't he give you any other reward?'

'He gave me money for a pilgrimage to Rome,' said Audun.

'King Svein gives money to lots of people,' said the King of Norway, 'even when they don't give him presents. Anything else?'

'He offered to make me a courtier and heap me with honours,' said Audun.

'That was a good offer. But I would have done more,' said King Harald.

'He also gave me a ship and all its cargo to sell here in Norway and Iceland.'

'That was a handsome present,' said King Harald. 'But I would have done the same. Anything else?'

'Yes,' said Audun, 'he also gave me a big purse of silver in case I lost the ship and cargo in a shipwreck.'

'That was generously done,' said King Harald. 'I wouldn't have done *that*. I would have decided we were even with the ship.'

'There was something else, sire,' said Audun. 'He also gave me this silver armlet and urged me never to give it away unless it was to some great man to whom I owed a great debt. And now I want to give it to you, sire, because you had the chance of keeping my bear for yourself and punishing me, but instead, you let me go free to give a fine gift to your enemy.'

The King of Norway accepted the gift most graciously, and gave Audun magnificent presents in exchange. And Audun left for Iceland, and went home to his mother. Audun lived nearly a thousand years ago, but the story of Audun and his polar bear is still remembered and told in Iceland today.

from ICELANDIC STORIES

ALGY MET A BEAR

Anonymous

Algy met a bear;
The bear met Algy.
The bear grew bulgy;
The bulge was Algy.